The Pixum Papers

The Pixum Papers

Nine TAILS and One DOGGEREL

Transcribed from the Journals

of

Mr Podmore PIXUM

[with a few ephemeric jottings from Mr Bertie Fox]

by

WILLIAM J BOOKER

MGC

Published in 2019 by Maddox Gryphon Cornet

Previously published in 2018 by KDP

ISBN 978-1-5272-5458-9

Previously published privately for limited circulation.
All texts revised © William J Booker 2018.

Ill Met By Moonlight (2009)
The Walking Tour (2017)
The Tale of The Tail of The Dark and the Head of the Tale of the Heart of The Light (2000)
A Fool's Errant (2002)
One Last Summer at World's End (2003)
Twice Bitten, Once Shy (2006)
Let Every Eye Negotiate (2016)
The Lost Boy (2004)
The Box (2010)
The Crispness of a Camel (2008)

Cover design, illustrations, typography
and layout by the author.

Foreword

England, in the world in which Mr Pixum chooses to inhabit most of the time, is contemporaneous with the world in which most of us choose to live. It appears to be set, by our terms of reference, in the 18th Century — or maybe the early 19th Century. Who can tell? Probably a mixture of both. There are many similarities to what we know of those periods in our history but, make no mistake—there are differences also, as you will discover.

It has been theorised that each time we have choices to make we create a new universe—or series of univi—in which all possible outcomes of those choices play themselves out. If that is the case, then consensus of thought in Mr Pixum's England, and by extension, his world, has continued to make some rather wise choices. You can feel a kind of "natural sanity" here—at least some of the time. Certainly a quality of life maintains, testimony to the quality of thought, decisions—and The Feathers of Fate—operating here. But as we know, change is a constant . . .

Caveat Lector

Discerning Reader, although they stand alone, there are some instances of continuity from one story to the next, therefore, may I advise you to read them in the order in which they are here presented?

CONTENTS

Ill Met By Moonlight

From the window, the fox watched carriages and carts vying for space in the street. This early and already bustling, people hurrying in every direction, all of them apparently late for something or other. It would become even busier as the day found its feet. At each end of the street, the haphazard frontages of buildings gradually faded away into autumn mist. Across the street, above a sea of rooftops, though, he could see the palest blue, a tint of the clear sky to come once the sun rose higher and became strong enough to chase away this carpet of fallen cloud.

Behind him he heard the homely sounds of coal spitting in the grate and the crunch his friend's teeth made as they bit into a slice of toast.

Returning his gaze to the hurly-burly in the street, he could not help but be aware of the purpose that radiated in waves from the clanking and clattering, the shouts and whinnies, the relentless *activity* down below. Mr Bertie Fox compared this with the doldrums of his own life these past few months and felt a sense of being out of things, out of the world in which things *happen*, although paradoxically, he felt no guilt whatsoever about living a life of leisure. He was a fox who was normally content to let the world go by, whether he was watching it or no. He was happy to save his energy for his forays into Society, immaculately turned out and sparkling with wit and joviality, taking as much pleasure in being seen at all the best places as he did from savouring the cuisine, the fine wines and the prettiest vixens London had to offer. With a French father, an English mother, and having spent the first several years of his life *dans le Royaume de France*, his breeding served to heighten his aesthetic appreciation of the good things in life.

Just lately, though, he'd experienced a sinking of the spirit now the nights, coming down ever earlier as the planet sped from Equinox to Winter Solstice, signified nothing more than the end of another day passing without change. What was new? Nothing. What was stimulating? Nothing. Glancing back over his shoulder, he saw his friend, Mr Podmore Pixum, sitting by the fire, munching toast and reading. *He* seemed content at any rate. Never more satisfied than with his head in a book, which, to the fox, seemed to be rather too often—Bertie Fox was not a fellow to whom being ignored was acceptable, and he resented the fact that Pixum, who was supposed to be his friend, evidently thought he was.

He flung himself back into the chair on the opposite side of the hearth to Mr Pixum, plucked up *The Times* from where he'd left it on the arm and shook it out in such a manner that even he, the urbane Bertie Fox, thought petulant. The simple truth was that he was bored.

"Pigs In Parlour, Farmer In Sty," said the headline. Pah! Blether was blether, whether in ink or in air. Page two, blah, blah. Why in Hermes' name do they think anyone in their right mind would be interested in any of this? Political catfights, fraudulent financiers. Blah. That slice of toast smells heavenly. Water in mouth—be dribbling soon. *Carpe* toast! Grab it! Oh *no*!

Just as Mr Fox's white-gloved hand reached out with lightning speed and was within a whisker of the golden round—the *last* golden round—Mr Pixum, without taking his eye from whatever paragraph was occupying his attention and without apparent awareness of the fox's intent, and also with the most indolent of actions, removed the toast in a blink and champed it between his teeth.

Petulance was too mild a word: Bertie Fox shook the newspaper with such force that on the third shake several pages broke loose from his grip and drifted onto the hearthrug. He scowled.

'Here we are,' he thought, 'two thirds of the Feathers of Fate and for months the Arrow of Destiny shows not the slightest wobble. Me twiddling my thumbs, going quietly mad; him over there with his nose permanently in the pages of some book . . . Hello . . . What was that?'

From down beside his chair Mr Pixum produced a plate.

'Last, last slice,' he said, 'If you want it?'

Warmth glowed around Mr Fox's heart for a brief moment. His friend's kindness was touching—or would have been had he not offered Mr Fox a piece of charcoal that he had himself rejected some time ago.

The Arrow of Destiny, that great universal, nay, multiversal, ideal that carries, directs and ensures the path of flourishing cosmic health through existence as a whole—and through this fairly local continuum of dimensions (or this Vale of Tears as some cynics would have it)—is deemed by Higher Orders of Beings (each level of which is a triumvirate), to require an occasional nudge back on course should the need arise. Each conscious act of a wilfully destructive, negative nature creates dissonance in the Great Symphony of the Cosmoses, it can loosen a button on the tail-coat of the First Cause. Every part of All-That-Is is of equal import, from univi, galaxies, planets (and other worlds) to a cartwheel, a cobweb, a door knocker, a spoon, a molecule or a quantum of energy; scale counts for nothing. The Feathers of Fate, of which those we currently speak are but one of several groups of three members, are specially chosen by the lowest of the Higher Orders for their unique qualities, this last represented to our trio as one Sonny Tiphareth.* The name, Feathers of Fate (continuing the archerial symbolism of the Arrow of Destiny), derives from the fletchings, or flight feathers, of an arrow, usually three in number, and whose function it is to ensure its smooth trajectory. One of the feathers is known as the Cock Feather, that being the designation of Mr Fox's friend, Mr Pixum.

The fox, scrabbling up the loose news-sheets, had happened upon a heading that appeared somewhere within the run of the newspaper instead of blurting from the front page or indeed, the second or third pages. It read:

SIR ROGER AND LADY QUARTERHAWSE

DISAPPEAR IN

LOCKED ROOM MYSTERY

Any one of these would have been enough to catch the eye of the excitement-deprived Mr Fox: "Disappear," "Locked Room," and, the most alluring word of all, "Mystery," and to have them appear all together was the equivalent of a raptor flush in a game of whistle. Mr Fox's first thought upon digesting this tasty morsel (which, for the moment, was a poor substitute for the toast) was, 'Just another enticing banner making much of nothing.'

Surprisingly, the report held good as far as it went:

SIR ROGER and LADY QUARTERHAWSE are reported to be missing from their home, Woodscott House, in the County of Surrey. Your correspondent has been informed that the wealthy couple was found to be absent from their usual rooms at four o'clock yesterday afternoon. Various household staff witnessed the QUARTERHAWSEs entering the room at that hour.

The facts appear to be thus: SIR ROGER and LADY QUARTERHAWSE, for reasons unknown, entered the study, locked themselves inside and simply disappeared. It has been ascertained that the room was locked from the inside. The study, situated on the ground floor to the rear of the house, was found to be unoccupied when the Head Gardener, a Mr Fawcett,

4

peered through the window. A thorough search of Woodscott House and grounds was conducted; no trace of the missing couple was found.

An eminent and respected member of parliament, SIR ROGER is well known in London Society as well as in his Home County of Surrey. LADY QUARTERHAWSE, reputedly descended from German aristocracy, is rarely seen at Social Events but is said to be very beautiful and sophisticated. The couple have no children to date.

Having folded the page to a manageable size, Mr Fox passed it over to Mr Pixum, and after 'tonging' a fresh lump of sea-coal onto the fire, sat tapping his toe on the hearth.

After several *Hmm . . . Hmm's*, Mr Pixum snapped to his feet, allowing the folded paper to fall to the rug in its own time. The sudden action startled the fox. He gasped.

'Despite your conclusions regarding my "bookish lifestyle," said Mr Pixum, mage, scholar and (cock) Feather of Fate, 'I do manage to keep myself limber.' His eye was a grey rapier piercing Mr Fox.

'I haven't—' began Mr Fox.

'Don't,' said Mr Pixum, twirling an admonitory finger, 'mire yourself further. No use pretending, my friend. I know that you know that I know exactly what you were thinking. Might as well admit it, but of course you will not, being such a stubborn fellow.'

Mr Pixum grinned.

Always, or almost always, quick to recover, Mr Fox curled the left side of his muzzle, exposing a little more incisor. Without moving his jaw he said, 'If you say so.'

His gaze remained intently unfocused upon a piece of air somewhere just short of the ceiling.

Eye a-sparkle and demeanour somewhere between something-more-than-perky and just-short-of-bouncy, Mr Pixum announced, 'Off we go then!'

He snatched up his coat, flung open the door and roared down the stairwell, 'Mrs Enderby!'

Without awaiting a reply, he followed his words downstairs, with Mr Fox, dapper as ever, at his heels.

At just after one o'clock in the afternoon of that same day, in the village of Scopwick Green, three travellers settled close to a blazing fire in the Three Owls, a half-timbered inn, of which time had contrived successfully to deprive each constituent timber of any parallel qualities as well as any angle in the region of ninety degrees it may once have had in its relationship to its fellows.

How they found the village was a mystery to Mr Fox. As far as he knew, the only direction they had been given (this from a brewer they met on the turnpike) was, 'It's nowhere near Godalming.'

'Poddy can be a clever sort sometimes,' thought the fox.

Pipes primed, spills lit from the fire, ale served.

Despite the beams of light that the autumn sun shot through leaded lights, the interior of the inn, on some ancient and perverse whim, managed to gather its shadows into itself, as if they were a collection of black ostrich feathers, and use them to preserve a mysterious twilight. The room, perfumed with the aroma of wood smoke, was an altogether agreeable place from which to embark upon an adventure, if such this turned out to be.

'A most congenial establishment,' observed the man with pointed ears and wearing a top hat, 'set in a delightful village.'

'We like to think so.'

The innkeeper, a stout woman of some fifty winters by the name of F. Bagnell (if indeed, it was she whose name was painted on the lintel above the entrance), accepted the compliment with a nod. Her expression, should any astute traveller care to read beneath the fifty blizzards of face powder and her attempt to impersonate a barn door, would reveal that oft-seen mixture of suspicion and calculation so familiar to strangers when visiting a country inn.

Three astute strangers read beneath.

In as much of an undertone as he could manage, given that his voice in normal tones possessed the subtle orchestration of a rusty hinge, the creaking of roof timbers in a gale and granite being pulverised by a mortar and pestle, the diminutive gentleman, his head adorned by an upturned teapot, the glaze of which reflected the flames of ash logs, said, 'Beneath that idyllic appearance lies a peculiarity for which, at present, I cannot identify the cause.'

His eyes, which also caught the glint of firelight, swivelled to each of his companions as he applied a spill to the bowl of his pipe and puffed.

Whether this last remark referred to the landscape or the landlady, was unclear. His two companions exchanged glances and smiled. Food for thought, but at that particular moment it lacked sufficient sauce to pique their appetite.

The wearer of the red Teapot was none other than the legendary Teapot Man, Student of Destiny and third Feather of Fate. Mr Pixum and Mr Fox had collected him from his lodgings before heading southeast and arranging accommodation at the Three Owls.

The companionable silence in which the trinity sat and smoked was interrupted only by the occasional rumble from Mr Fox's stomach: both silence and rumble were terminated by the arrival at their table of the parlour-boy bearing a tray of game pie and hot loaves.

Upon entering the inn, Mr Pixum had formed the impression that he and his friends were alone in the parlour, but during the course of the meal, as his eye roved about the murky room, he eventually, and with some slight alarm, discerned the telltale shapes of waistcoat buttons, lapels and finally a nose, all of which added up to the presence of another occupant. He took a surreptitious peep through his Magick Eye, letting the patch fall back into place. The glimpse revealed nothing noteworthy; in a recent investigation, an incident had left the Eye's power much diminished. The newly-discovered personage had the appearance of a rustic gentleman of portly build, probably a local man with a kindly, simple face. Nothing suspicious.

As they stood preparatory to taking their leave, the innkeeper asked, 'I expect you gentlemen have urgent business to attend?'

An impertinent question, thought Mr Pixum, but in rural areas folk were often used to knowing each other's affairs and were less constrained than those of more gracious manners.

'Nothing of the sort,' he replied, 'we are here for pleasure only. We thought to take a stroll in Scophurst Wood and enjoy the air.'

The innkeeper's look of disapproval belied her words.

'The woods are lovely, especially at this time of year. Autumn is such a beautiful season if the weather holds. I'm sure you'll have an enjoyable afternoon.'

'Make sure you're back on the highway afore nightfall.'

These words, uttered by the hitherto silent gent in the corner, took them by surprise.

'Whatever do you mean?' Mr Fox responded, 'Why should we be worried about being in the woods after dark?'

'Haunted,' said the man, looking comfortable, legs stretched out, tankard balanced on his belly. 'Reputed to be.'

F. Bagnell raised her painted brows.

'Throtespear, gents,' he said, thrusting out a hand, 'Horace Throtespear.'

'It's only a ghost story,' said the innkeeper, quickly, 'You know how these places attract stories. The stag barks, clouds hide the moon, the screech of a . . . erm . . .'

'Fox?' asked Mr Fox.

'Mm . . . Owl,' said the innkeeper, 'Next thing you know . . . folk are saying what they saw . . .'

'Tis more than a hold howl,' said Throtespear from his corner, 'Folk've died there. She's been seen floating about in the trees.'

'Died? Seen?' said Mr Fox.

F. Bagnell, innkeeper, said, 'People have been found dead there. These things happen, they . . .'

'Killed,' said Horace, 'Throats torn out. And that's the recent dead.'

'There are more?' asked Mr Pixum.

'Just one I know'd of. It'd be just over two, two and a half year ago now.'

'Who was killed? Was the murderer caught?'

'Sir Roger's daughter, it was. Killed the same as them others.' The man took a deep breath and let it out slowly. 'You can't catch a ghost. Or ghoul. Or vampyre.'

The innkeeper's mouth was a line tight with disapproval. 'That's nothing but superstitious rubbish. Simple folk will believe anything.'

Mr Pixum asked her, 'You don't believe?'

'Of course not! Just tales talked about at the fireside when the nights draw in. Some folk enjoy putting the shivers up each other's spines. That's all it is.'

Mr Pixum turned his attention to the man in the corner.

'Ghost, ghoul or vampyre? Have you any idea which of these it might be, assuming it's any of them?'

'No use asking me. I ain't seen none of 'em. I only heard tell of what other folks' been sayin'.'

'Sir Roger,' said Mr Fox, 'Who is he?'

'Sir Roger Quarterhawse. Q-u-a-r-t-e-r-h-a-w-s-e. You must've heard of him. Local bigwig, MP. Lives up the road aways, near Scophurst Woods. Kicked up a right ol' rumpus when his daughter got her throat . . . Dragged in the army and all sorts.'

Mr Pixum was surprised to hear Throtespear pronounce "Quarterhawse" as "Case."

'Who claims to have seen this ghost or whatever it is?' asked Mr Pixum.

'Locals, sir. A-walkin' in the woods after dark. And why? Up to no good, I'spect. Poachers. Young lovers. Word soon gets around. "Sad Annie," they calls her.'

'"Sad Annie"? The ghost is known as a she? Someone must have seen her,' said Mr Pixum.

'Hard to say who saw what, once the rumours started. Sir Roger thinks it's to do with Strype.'

'Strype?'

'S-t-r-y-p-e, Strype. Bad lot. Lives in a creepy old place deep in the woods, Woodfold Bower. Nasty business, all of it.'

'Nasty business?' Mr Fox asked, 'Who is this Strype?'

'I've said enough,' said Throtespear getting to his feet with an effort, 'I'll bid you good day.' He tipped his hat and left.

Mr Fox and Mr Pixum turned to The Teapot Man, who had remained silent during what had been, to all intents, an interrogation. The Teapot Man, with a nod, motioned that it was time to go and investigate.

'Enjoy your outing,' said the innkeeper, who had accompanied them outside.

'I think,' said Mr Pixum, climbing aboard the chaise and taking the reins from the ostler, 'it will be a splendid afternoon for sightseeing.'

As Mr Fox approached, Archie the horse became restive, as he had when setting off from London.

'*Ils n'ont pas besoin d'être effrayés,*' said Mr Fox, '*Je n'apprécie pas la viande chevaline.*'

'Your scent gives him the willies,' said Mr Pixum.

'I'm not surprised,' said the fox, 'I bought it in Paris.'

Woodscott House, the Quarterhawse residence, was situated on the right hand side of the road, some distance from the village. When eventually they drew up at the gates, they saw wooded hills rising in the distance, waves of gold fading away into the purple of late afternoon, but of the house itself, there was no sign. On either side of the gates stood a lodge. The gates were chained and locked. Through the gates, a tree-lined drive wound into a clump of trees. Before any of the three companions alighted, the door of the left hand lodge opened and out stepped a soldier, his rifle at high port. Without preamble, he snapped, 'State your business!'

Remembering to use the correct pronunciation, Mr Pixum duly stated, 'We're visiting Sir Roger Quarterhawse, sergeant.'

'No visitors today, sir,' said the soldier, 'The whole estate is out-of-bounds. Staff sent away.'

'May we ask why?' asked Mr Pixum politely, 'Is there anything we can do to help, perhaps?'

'You may ask, sir,' replied the soldier, his scarlet tunic glowing in the sunshine as if with its own internal light, 'Unfortunately I cannot give an answer.' Possibly as an afterthought, he added, 'Orders, sir.'

'Whatever has occurred in this place, that the military is set on guard at the gates?' mused Mr Pixum, as if talking to himself, 'Presumably because Sir Roger is an elected member of the English Parliament. Surely the constable should deal with any unfortunate event this close to Scopwick Green?'

'I wouldn't know, sir. I was ordered down from Guildford yesterday. "None may enter." Nothing about no constables, sir.'

Mr Pixum let his gaze wander over the gates, over the twin lodges flanking them and over the bosky acres beyond, finally coming to rest upon the soldier. Affecting a look of disappointment, he said, 'Well, this is all very distressing. I do hope it's nothing too serious.' He shook the reins. 'Good afternoon to you, sergeant.'

The soldier stood and watched them as they trotted the chaise down the road and disappeared around a bend.

They stood on the hill, looking out through the trees of Scophurst Wood, catching their breath. It had been a steep climb over roots and through brushwood but the prospect was magnificent; the woods tumbled downhill and ended abruptly, giving way to the parkland surrounding Woodscott House. It rolled out before them, dotted with single trees: oak, ash, cedar. There were also stands of beech perched upon hillocks. Woodscott House squatted in a declivity, its gables and chimneys rising above the trees.

Mr Pixum had no need to explain his plan to his colleagues, they understood the situation as well as he. Together, they descended through the wood in the direction of the great house.

'He seems to make a circuit of the buildings every half hour or so,' said Mr Fox, basing this statement on the fact that they had watched the soldier make two such rounds during the hour and a quarter in which they had been observing the house. They were hidden inside some rhododendron bushes, a hundred yards from the south-eastern corner of the house. Daylight was draining away and a pale moon had risen clear of the trees.

'Then it's time to make our move,' said Mr Pixum. 'Remember, the newspaper account has it that the Quarterhawses disappeared from a locked room *to the rear* of the house.'

They covered the distance to the corner of the building and crept around the back, keeping to a gravel path. The windows were just low enough for Mr Pixum, on tip-toe, to peep through, and by the skulking light of a dark lantern, he was able to form an idea of the contents of each room. The first room was decorated in the Venetian style with wreaths in recesses and a marble floor, the next was huge—he could see only a small area— it looked like a ballroom, predominantly red, with silken cushions and gold leaf aplenty. In the next room stood a pedestal desk and the walls were lined with books: unmistakably a study. Mr Pixum stood back from the window and closed the lantern. In the last few minutes the dark had advanced. The remaining brightness lay to the west.

'We need something upon which to stand,' said Mr Pixum, 'The sill is too high for us to climb in.'

There was nothing nearby that would do for their purpose. The

Teapot Man spotted a large wall to the east of the formal garden.

'The walled garden. The gardener will need a ladder to tend the fruit trees.'

'If a ladder is there, I'm the owl to find it,' said Mr Fox, 'I have excellent night vision.'

'What of the soldier?' asked The Teapot Man.

'We must look out for him, obviously,' said Mr Pixum, 'He is, after all, armed. If there is a chance of him discovering us, our only course of action is to attack first.'

'Somewhat harsh, isn't it?' asked Mr Fox, 'He's only following orders.'

'It is logical to commence with an attack: it cuts out all the fuzzy details and allows us to achieve our objective.'

'We become the aggressors, attacking without first attempting some form of negotiation, diplomacy . . ?'

'We know that would be a waste of time. It would merely forewarn and thus forearm him. We'll make no progress by standing at the wrong end of a rifle.'

The moon had ascended further, revealing their surroundings in the deceptive way that only moonlight at twilight can. Mr Pixum and The Teapot Man crouched by a low hedge and watched Mr Fox glide across the lawns, run along paths through the formal garden and finally vanish into the shadows of the garden wall. Somewhere in the woods an owl hooted.

'Damn!' said Mr Fox to himself as he tried the main gate into the garden and found it locked. He could smell fresh oil on the lock mechanism and keyhole. There was nothing for it but to circle the wall and hope to find another means of ingress. He was conscious of how little time was left before the soldier would return on his tour of sentry duty.

The walled garden obviously covered a large area, which meant his journey around the perimeter would use up valuable time. He negotiated his way as quietly as he could along gravel paths, through shrubberies and around assorted statuary. At last he arrived at the back wall. As he approached the half way point, to his relief he found a small door set into the stone. To his greater relief he found it unlocked. The hinges groaned. Without hesitation, he entered.

He found himself looking across an expanse of freshly tilled beds lying fallow for the winter. Along one side, rows of fruit trees were espaliered against the full length of the wall, on the other side stood several glass houses, but what caught his attention was the building set in the farthest corner, next to the main gate. The moonlight made it easy for him to dash along the uncluttered pathway. When he arrived at the building he found it to be locked. A glance through cobwebby panes told him it was a potting shed and general store for gardening implements. There were racks of tubers against the far wall but no sign of a ladder. To one side of the brick shed, a clutter of planks and a huge door leaned against the wall. The fox leapt over some large plant pots to get a closer look; alas, he was not nimble enough. He caught the toe of his boot on a pot and the pot keeled over, smashing into its neighbour.

The fox froze. What was that? His ears pricked up. He thought he'd heard . . . Yes, he had! The unmistakable crunch of boot on gravel. He took a deep calming breath and assessed the situation. This was obviously part of the sentry's round. He may not have heard the pot breaking. He may not have heard the hinges of the garden gate. He had a rifle . . .

Exercising caution, Mr Fox tiptoed over to the leaning door. Perhaps he could hide behind it? The whole corner, he saw, was untidy, a graveyard for broken wheelbarrows, rusty sieves and other assorted articles that had reached the end of their usefulness. He peered gingerly behind the door into impenetrable darkness. Feeling his way, he slipped into the gap and grasped . . . a rung! Oh success! He could climb the ladder up one side of the wall, pull it up and climb down the other. He listened for a full minute but heard no further sounds from the soldier. He grasped the ladder and yanked. It came out from behind the door with hardly any resistance, but unfortunately two of the planks became dislodged.

They wasted no time in falling against the potting shed and smashing the window.

It was all up now. There was nothing to gain by stealth. The ladder was about eight feet long. With hardly a sound Mr Fox carried it to the wall and climbed it to the top. He carefully peeked over... and saw the soldier waiting below. There was something crafty in his manner.

'Two can play that game,' he thought, carefully descending the ladder. He struggled back to the top with his burden, lodged it briefly on the coping while he made sure of his footing, and then carefully took aim.

From their position by the hedge, Mr Pixum and The Teapot Man were startled by a crash followed swiftly by a scraping sound. There was a minute of silence before they heard a commotion in the formal garden and then Mr Fox appeared, dragging a ladder across the lawn.

Mr Pixum asked in a low voice, 'What was all that noise?'

'No need to whisper!' said the fox, 'I was forced to consider your philosophical advice. On the spur of the moment I put it into action. The sentry's out cold and bound with gardening twine.'

He hefted the ladder against the window, resting the top against the horizontal bar of the sash frame, climbed halfway up and kicked in one of the lowest panes. He then climbed down, lowered the top of the ladder to the sill, climbed up once more and, unfastening the window-latch, lifted the sash and climbed inside, his brush flowing gracefully behind him.

Mr Pixum and The Teapot Man looked at each other and nodded. Once Bertie Fox got his teeth into something, there really was no stopping him.

The dark lantern revealed more of what they had discerned from outside. The study was spacious and quite shabby. There was dust everywhere. The desk was of oak, large and heavy. There was a chair to match. Book-lined walls. Some apparatus, possibly alchemical, possibly not. Mr Pixum, a practitioner himself, had certainly not seen the like before. Most unusual. There was also a bureau, a terrestrial globe, a table painted in blue with a gold trim that had some loose jewellery scattered on its surface, a fireplace and a large chest.

Mr Pixum examined the door. It remained locked from the inside. They began a systematic search of the room. They found no clues among the papers on the desk or in the drawers—they all pertained either to Sir Roger's political affairs or his household accounts. Inside the chest, curiously, they found half a loaf of bread, two fresh apples and a jug of water. They pulled back the Persian rug but found no sign of a trapdoor. A careful tap around the walls and fireplace revealed no hidden panels or sliding doors. This was a puzzle.

The jewellery on the table was odd. It was a woman's jewellery, scattered as if thrown down carelessly. The Teapot Man, as is his wont, was happily examining the texture of the floorboards and the grain of the desk.

Mr Pixum realised he'd repeatedly returned to the table with the jewellery. He tapped The Teapot Man's shoulder and nodded towards the table.

'Egyptian?'

The Teapot Man made a clicking sound in his throat.

'Most peculiar, but no. There's something . . .' He stooped to examine the legs. 'I've seen tables with lion's feet and ball-and-claw feet but I've never seen anything like this.'

Mr Pixum shone the dark lantern closer. Strange indeed. The table had stylised human feet at the end of its legs. Two of the legs. The other two legs ended in stylised human hands . . . A drawer bulged out of the front. Mr Pixum reached out to open it but The Teapot Man stayed his arm.

'Wait!' He ran his fingers along the edges and felt beneath, then turned to his friend with a gleam in his eye.

'Leave this to me,' he said.

He fumbled in his coat pockets and pulled out a small teapot.

'I hope this does the trick,' he said, 'because it's all I have to hand.'

He removed the lid, sniffed the contents and replaced it, seemingly satisfied.

'Stand back,' he said, 'because, gentlemen, if my assumption is correct . . .'

He stood by the table, held the miniature teapot above it and proceeded to pour out some fine powder just as if he was pouring a cup of tea.

There was a bang and a crack. The Feathers of Fate stepped farther away. The table began to lurch back and forth, emitting a series of groans and squeaks. It began to shudder with some violence, the wood bending, the cracks becoming louder.

'By the tufted tail of—' Before Mr Pixum could finish his oath a woman stood before them, fully clothed, wearing a dress of blue trimmed with gold. She pushed her hands into the small of her back and winced then swept the three companions with a glare. Mr Pixum said, 'Madam, I—'

'I am Lady Quarterhawse,' snapped the woman, gathering up the jewellery, 'Who, may I ask, are you?'

Mr Pixum observed a human female of great beauty, still in the flush of youth, with golden hair and blue eyes, but it was a cold beauty. Here was a woman possessed of elegance and arrogance. In her eyes he saw no mercy, no forgiveness.

He introduced himself and his two friends and went on to explain to her, in a calm and clear fashion, why they were there and what had happened. This news brought about an instant transformation in Lady Quarterhawse. The haughtiness drained away and she swayed on her feet. Mr Fox helped her to a chair.

'Please forgive me,' she said, 'I have had something of an ordeal. I can hardly believe . . .' She put her head in her hands. 'Two days? This is all a dream, surely?'

'Not a dream,' said The Teapot Man, 'Minutes ago you were an occasional table.'

'Occasional?' A hint of ice returned to her voice but it was quickly smothered when a new realisation became evident in her expression. 'But where is Sir Roger? M-My husband?' She turned away.

Mr Pixum spoke gently. 'We found only yourself, my Lady.'

'Do you have any recollection of what happened?' asked The Teapot Man.

'None. I . . . Oh, wait! Yes . . . It's becoming clearer. Strype! It was Strype! Oh, what has become of my husband?'

'Please be calm,' said Mr Pixum, 'and tell us what you know. We will do all we can to find Sir Roger.'

'Oberon Strype. He called upon Sir Roger. I-It was unusual. He had never called upon us before. There is some bad feeling between us. My husband brought him in here.' With a gesture, her hands took in the study. 'Before many minutes had passed, I heard raised voices. Alarmed, I came in to find out what the trouble was.'

She looked at them, tears flowing freely.

'Strype was threatening my husband with a dagger. Sir Roger said he would never part with the Helm. Strype threatened his life. When he saw me, he ran to the door and locked it. I had a spare key and made to escape but he knocked me aside.'

'Helm?' Mr Pixum and Mr Fox asked in unison.

'I need to tell you the whole story,' said Lady Quarterhawse, and she proceeded to do so.

Oberon Strype, she said, lived in a house deep in Scophurst Wood. It had been his parents' house and Strype had remained there alone after they died.

Sir Roger's daughter from his first marriage, Mona, along with two other people, had been killed. Sir Roger believed Strype to be the murderer. This was never proven. The coroner reached a verdict of "death by assailant or assailants unknown" in all three cases. It was believed by some of the locals that "Sad Annie" had done away with them all. Nevertheless, Sir Roger hated Strype, who was thought, in any event, to be "strange."

Sir Roger had attended a ball at the Rafferty's of Wellover Hall, where, unfortunately, Strype had also been invited. The Quarter-hawses thought this to be a breach of etiquette on the part of the Raffertys, as they surely knew how things stood between Sir Roger and Strype. However, Sir Roger overheard something of interest on that night.

Strype's father had been a traveller and a collector; one item he had brought home from his travels was part of an ancient Anglo-Saxon artefact known as the Helm of Gagnir, said to have belonged to Utlac, a friend of Wiglac of the Geats, who helped Beowulf slay the dragon. Utlac found the Helm in the dragon's hoard after Beowulf's death and took it as a prize with Wiglac's permission. It was said to confer upon the wearer the ability to locate hidden treasure—a runic inscription inside the Helm stated that it worked only if accompanied with the two Dragon's Claws, which had to be fitted into the sockets provided: completed, it resembled a horned Anglo-Saxon helmet. Strype's father had reason to believe the Claws were somewhere in England. Unfortunately, he never found them.

Now, Sir Roger, who was sitting quietly in an alcove in the Hall, overheard this story accidentally. When he heard Strype boasting that he was "within a whisker" of obtaining the fabled Claws, he began to simmer. How could he let the man who had murdered his daughter succeed in his quest? Was it fair that Strype should not only get away with murder, but also have the means to acquire enormous wealth simply by donning a wretched old helmet?

In the event, fortune smiled upon Sir Roger for, some months later, he attended an auction at Trowbridge Eels and found the Helm to be one of the lots. There were no other bidders. Sir Roger couldn't believe his luck. Once the Helm was safely locked away in Woodscott House he wasted no time ensuring Strype came to know of his coup. Sir Roger wanted to taunt Strype with the fact that the Helm was now forever unattainable to him. It was, at least, a form of revenge and Sir Roger was content with it. Her husband, claimed Lady Quarterhawse, admitted it was a decidedly immature thing to do, but the deed was done and he was nevertheless satisfied with the outcome.

What the Quarterhawses had not imagined was that the covetous Strype would call at their house. Nor had they imagined he would burst in and threaten their lives, steal the Helm and transform Lady Quarterhawse into an occasional table as a final flourish, before somehow making his exit from a locked room – locked from the inside. Where was Sir Roger? She had no idea. Oh, and didn't she mention that Strype was reputed to be an accomplished sorcerer, which might explain how this feat was effected? The theft of the Helm suggested Strype had also gained possession of the Claws.

When Lady Quarterhawse had finished her account, Mr Pixum's first words were, 'Such a cheap method of deception, sorcery—the expedient route most frequently taken by scoundrels, scoundrels with enough self-discipline and vision to make it work. Fortunately there are so few of them.'

Crackling through stalks of dead cow parsley that resembled dry bones in the moonlight, Mr Pixum led the other two Feathers of Fate back into Scophurst Wood. They had decided to beard Strype in his den, having left Lady Quarterhawse with the promise that they would do all within their power to find Sir Roger and the Helm.

They strode the woodland path in silence, the moonlight giving every shadow a double meaning. All that remained of the setting sun, visible through the trees, was a stripe of blue and pink along the horizon. Occasionally they would hear rustlings among the trees or the hoot of an owl far-off in the darkness. Mr Pixum was feeling decidedly vulnerable and he and Mr Fox both gasped when The Teapot Man suddenly blurted,

'Do you feel them?'

Annoyed, Mr Pixum asked, 'Feel what?'

'The Threads of Destiny,' replied The Teapot Man, 'I can feel them so strongly that I presumed the pull was enough that even the two of you would be able to feel it.' He stopped walking and said, 'Be warned. There is something ghastly afoot.'

'Reassuring,' said Mr Fox.

Feeling ever more uneasy, they continued deeper into the wood.

It was when crossing a clearing, the moonlight depicting the fallen leaves as a silver-grey carpet, that Mr Fox, in a harsh whisper, said, 'See over there!'

He pointed to where the woods swept uphill from the clearing's edge. Mr Pixum and The Teapot Man followed his white-gloved finger and saw her . . .

Among the first rank of oaks stood the willowy figure of a girl. Straight dark hair framed a face painted white by the light of the moon. She wore woodland clothes, a belted tunic and leggings.

'*Par la théière sacrée!*' exclaimed Mr Fox.

'"*Alone and palely loitering,*"' quoted The Teapot Man. 'So it's true then.'

'So it seems,' said Mr Pixum in a hushed voice, 'The legend of Sad Annie is alive and well after all.'

'I can feel her melancholy,' said The Teapot Man.

'*Don't stare at her!*' Mr Pixum hissed quietly, 'She may be dangerous. Remember the murders!' He strode off across the clearing without another glance. His companions followed him, making haste as slowly as they dared, lest they disturb the mysterious shade.

Eventually, after what seemed several hundred yards, they picked up a stream to their right and simply followed it until the path veered upwards and away. As they crested the slope they saw a clear trackway leading off to their left.

'Woodfold Bower, I'll wager,' said Mr Fox.

They turned onto the track.

Soon they spotted a light some distance ahead and, as the track descended into a brake of ash, they had their first sight of the home of Oberon Strype.

Neither a modest cottage nor a grand house, Woodfold Bower

was, however, a dwelling of more than middling dimensions. There was the dome of an observatory on the roof and what looked like a small graveyard to the right.

Mr Pixum lifted the knocker from the jaws of some mythical beast cast in bronze and let it fall. They heard the thud reverberate through the house. Then, silence.

'I don't like this,' said Mr Fox, looking nervously about and snuffling the air, 'We should be armed.'

'Courage, my friend,' said Mr Pixum, letting go of the knocker once again. This time, before the reverberations had died away, the sound of footsteps could be heard approaching from within. Bolts were drawn. The door opened.

'Good evening,' said a voice from the shadows, 'A strange sort of time for a visit. Are you lost?'

'Do we have the pleasure of addressing Mr Strype? Mr Oberon Strype?' asked Mr Pixum politely.

'You are correct in that particular,' said the voice, 'even if you are lost.'

'Far from lost, sir,' replied Mr Pixum, 'Far from *that*. We have urgent business we would discuss with you.'

'Oh dear. You are serious. I'm not sure I like the implications of this. Upon my life I cannot think what "urgent business" you could possibly have with me.'

'Our business,' said Mr Pixum sternly, 'concerns the disappearance of a neighbour of yours, along with a valuable item of his property. What can you tell us, Mr Strype?'

'N-Neighbour? We—I have no neighbours.'

'Surely, sir, you know of whom we speak? Sir Roger and Lady Quarterhawse?'

'Oh. Them.'

'Yes, sir, "Them."' Stepping closer to the door. 'Sir Roger has disappeared. Most likely abducted. His wife has been treated abominably. I repeat, sir, *what can you tell us?*'

A sigh. 'I know absolutely nothing of the fate of Sir Roger Quarterhawse or the treatment of his wife. The farthest I have been from this house in what? Two months? Two and a half months? Yes, two and a half months, is a few hundred yards into the woods to forage. I'm afraid I can't help you.'

The door was closing. Mr Pixum put his boot into the jamb.

'I'm not at all satisfied with your explanation, Mr Strype. We will not leave until that condition is met.'

Another sigh. The door opened wide.

'You had better come inside then. It's too chill an evening to bicker on the doorstep.'

Oberon Strype sat by the fire. Mr Pixum, The Teapot Man and Mr Fox, sat wherever they could, given the mismatched collection of furniture, none of it designed to be sat upon. Strype had taken them on a tour of the house, including the cellars, the rooftop observatory (which had been closed up for some time, judging by the look of it) and the grounds, in order to prove he was not holding Sir Roger captive. Mr Pixum, while descending the stairs, had inadvertently brushed against Strype and had received a most peculiar sensation; in fact it was more of a vision.

It began with a sense of the beginnings and endings of particular episodes in the life of mortal flesh. A choice, a decision, a course of action, once taken, produces changes with unforeseen results. Each of these changes Mr Pixum visualised as a kind of capsule encompassing many points of light (each point representing various incidents and sub-decisions), each such capsule he saw in a different colour. If he thought about time as linear, the capsules were threaded like beads on a string; in a three dimensional model they appeared as drops of dew on a spider's web.

The trappings of an individual life, the dense physical world of land and sky, seasons and sunsets, streets and woodland, clothes and furniture, taverns and teapothecaries' shops, flags cracking in a stiff breeze and rainwater giving a gloss varnish to cobble-stones —he saw all of this "life furniture" as so much creaking detritus revolving around and through those dewdrop capsules, incidental for the most part, to the fall of the dominoes clattering through time, set in motion by choices made, creating a complex pattern of interacting threads, all comprising the components of the process we call a life.

He looked into the pattern of this specific life and saw a hole through one side, as it were—and leaves of oak, ash and thorn, red, ochre and green, revolving together like a flock of starlings, wheeling into a spiral, forming a tunnel and spinning with increasing speed, the perception drawing Mr Pixum's own life into itself with a scouring action, stripping away layers from his very self, exposing ramparts of excuses, his subtle deceptions, the curtains of his magician's booth, his fondness for Stilton cheese and crusted port, his quickening at the sight of a pretty girl, his fear of spiders, his dread of accounting, his loathing of bores. Now it lay open his deeper self, revealing him as a tangle of roots sparking and cracking, now a constellation blazing in a sky rigid with frost, now a rush of air moist with living cells . . .

His late father, Oberon Strype told them, had brought home the Helm of Gagnir, certainly not the Dragon's Claws.

'I never have sought the Claws. I am content with my life as it is and have no need of any treasure,' he said. 'The Helm is not kept in the house but hidden in a safe place as I am aware such an item is sure to attract fortune hunters.'

Mr Pixum informed Strype of the events preceding their arrival at Woodfold Bower.

Strype, a handsome, dark-featured fellow with hair hanging in waves to his shoulders, took a lively interest in the story but could offer no explanation for Lady Quarterhawse's accusations. He wore a short black jacket with silver buttons that hung open to reveal an open-necked chemise of white silk, tight breeches with vertical stripes in black and white and knee-length boots of black leather.

'I can only conclude,' he said, 'that Lady Quarterhawse is either lying through her teeth or she remains ensorcelled.'

'We have been informed that you practice sorcery,' said The Teapot Man.

'Another misconception. My father was such a practitioner. I have never had any interest in the art and prefer to leave well alone.'

'What do you do with your time out here in the woods?' asked Mr Pixum.

'I am researching the history of this area,' he replied, 'It's rich and fascinating. I am also cataloguing the flora and fauna of the woods . . . with the help of an . . . assistant.'

His face clouded with, Mr Pixum thought, some unpleasant memory. As if to punctuate the moment, a puff of smoke emerged from the chimney and rolled lazily upwards, caressing the oaken mantel, scenting the room with the aroma of apple wood.

Mr Pixum was perplexed. He suspected his friends were, too. They sat and stared into the fire, deep in thought. He cast his mind back over the case so far:

Quarterhawse was certainly missing. The Helm was purportedly stolen from Woodscott House. Or it had never been in Woodscott House. Lady Quarterhawse had certainly been a table. Strype claimed to have no interest in the Claws. He had not stolen the Helm because he already owned it. Strype also denied having a hand in the death of Quarterhawse's daughter or of anyone else. Obviously this information did not add up. Someone was lying. What had the Quarterhawses to gain by accusing Strype of theft and murder? As far as he could work it out, nothing. What had Strype to gain by claiming the Helm was left to him by his father and that he did not own —nor seek to own—the Claws?

Any magistrate would definitely believe Quarterhawse over Strype. If Strype had stolen the Helm it were better if he claimed not to have it in his possession. And what of Sir Roger? Had Strype kidnapped him against the eventuality that he required a hostage? Hidden him in the woods? This was hopeless—so many questions and not one answer. Another thought sprang to his mind: Here they were, sitting with Oberon Strype, suspected murderer, thief and sorcerer—even now they could be sitting in a trap.

A movement caught his eye. Mr Fox was tapping his head with both hands. Of course! It was something they could do at that moment. They could allow Strype to prove he actually had the Helm in his possession.

Mr Pixum cleared his throat. 'Mr Strype,' he said, 'it would be a great help if you would be so kind as to show us the Helm.'

Strype came to with a start. 'Of course. Whenever it suits you. Just pop along one day and I'll be happy to oblige.'

'Now would suit us perfectly,' said Mr Pixum.

'N-Not now. No. Please come back tomorrow when we can see the path by daylight.' His hands clenched the arms of his chair. 'It's not the place to be walking at night. The wood, you know.'

Mr Pixum stood. 'Now, Mr Strype. Now!'

Strype led the way. He took them back along the path on which they had arrived but after a few hundred yards he turned off to the left, descended a steep slope then turned left again, until he stopped at an oak that was taller and broader than those surrounding it, its boughs jagged and writhing overhead.

The Teapot Man immediately began to study the patterns that the twigs and branches made across the face of the moon (It is his vocation to look for signs and portents in everything: years of experience have taught him the best places to focus his attention). He began to "collect" angles of branches, the curvature of arboreal bowers and the shapes made by the interlacing of twigs. Damp night air carried an aroma of humus and the exhalations of growing things. He held a leaf skeleton aloft: it resembled a dried out dryad.

Strype knelt before the oak, between roots as thick as his own body. Mr Pixum held up the dark lantern to give enough light for Strype to clear away a pile of dead leaves, revealing a slab hewn from sandstone. With his fingertips, he prised it up and heaved it to one side. The dark lantern's modest glow fell upon a staircase of rough wooden blocks.

'Follow me,' said Strype, disappearing below ground. With misgivings aplenty, Mr Pixum descended after him, followed by The Teapot Man. Mr Fox, his hackles bristling, paused a moment before taking the steps.

The room that opened out at the foot of the stairs was surprisingly spacious and the root-vaulted ceiling was high enough for them all to stand upright. Strype lit a couple of candles from the dark lantern, placing them in niches in the wall. Several crates and chests were stacked against the walls. All items of value to Oberon Strype, Mr Pixum guessed. Pulling out one of the chests, Strype inserted a key into the lid and opened it. Candlelight glimmered on the Helm. He lifted it from its bed of velvet and held it up. The quality of craftsmanship was obvious. There was a band around the base held in place with rivets and between each rivet a rune had been neatly engraved. On each side of the Helm a sturdy socket protruded. Strype handed it to Mr Pixum.

'What now?' he asked.

'At least we can vouch for its whereabouts,' mused Mr Pixum, stroking his chin, 'Perhaps it should remain here where it will be safe.'

'I think not,' said Strype, 'Forgive me if I don't entirely trust you . . . but you must understand my point of view. You could have told me a pack of lies. You could be agents sent by Sir Roger Quarterhawse. We could have been followed here.'

As they were, in fact, "agents sent" by Lady Quarterhawse, Mr Pixum made no comment.

'Where do you intend to take it?' asked Mr Fox.

'If I tell you that, I may as well leave it here,' said Strype reasonably.

There was no argument against that. When they emerged from underground, Strype handed the Helm to Mr Pixum to hold while he replaced the slab.

A great blast of air and smoke knocked them off their feet.

After a time, Mr Pixum opened his eye and saw only dense smoke with leaves fluttering about in it. He carefully checked his body for injuries and was pleased to find nothing more serious than a pain in his ribs. He became aware of the source of the pain: he had fallen on top of the Helm and was still lying on it. He rolled over and sat up. Through the thinning smoke he saw The Teapot Man and Mr Fox brushing themselves off. Of Oberon Strype there was no sign. Mr Fox re-lit the dark lantern and the trio made a cursory search of the area but found nothing.

'A guilty man, it seems,' said Mr Pixum, 'and I was almost ready to believe him, too.'

A sedentary life, though dull, thought the fox, at least posed no threat to the welfare of his wardrobe.

'Was that absolutely necessary?' he asked, 'I mean, he could've given us the slip any old way. I object quite strongly to this implied lack of respect for my clothing.'

'Take this to Lady Quarterhawse,' said Mr Pixum, handing the Helm to Mr Fox,

'Tell her we hope to find Sir Roger before too long. The news may lift her spirits.' He tilted back his top hat, scratched his head and addressed The Teapot Man. 'You and I need to take a closer look at Mr Strype's residence. Unless you have a better idea?'

The Teapot Man shook his head.

'Right then! Bertie, we'll meet you at Woodfold Bower. Farewell!'

The fox tucked the Helm under his arm and bounded away.

'Tally Ho!'

Bertie Fox's boots made barely a sound on the carpet of fallen leaves and soon faded away altogether.

Mr Pixum became aware of a rustling from behind him. He turned and saw The Teapot Man sitting cross-legged by the oak

tree's roots. He was busy fashioning something out of twigs by the light of the dark lantern. A closer inspection revealed a complex device constructed from small tree roots and twigs twisting in curlicues, forming a sphere roughly twelve inches in diameter. Within its structure were stars of struck silver and hollowed-out quartz globes lit from within with what Mr Pixum guessed was quintessence. He sat quietly down beside The Teapot Man and awaited developments.

Presently, the diminutive wearer of The Teapot seemed satisfied with his handiwork.

'Mm . . . Unph . . . Hmm,' he muttered to himself. Using forefinger and thumb he then proceeded to flick the sphere at various points. The flicks had the effect of making the quartz globes glow brighter and flicker. After a few more strategic flicks, the sphere began to emit a humming sound, at first fading and changing tone but eventually the glow and the tone stabilised, whereupon The Teapot Man rose to his feet and, with his attention focused upon the sphere, slowly rotated himself in a clockwise direction.

Mr Pixum stood away from him in the event his physical presence interfered in some way with the operation—whatever *that* was.

After a few minutes of patient revolution, The Teapot Man said, 'West-southwest.'

Mr Pixum, who had been miles away, working out parts of the syllabus for his New Year students, said, 'Eh?'

Swivelling his eyes Pixumwards, The Teapot Man allowed himself a triumphant grin. 'Sir Roger,' he said, 'is within half a mile of where we are now standing. Somewhere to the west-southwest.'

'Remarkable,' said Mr Pixum, nonplussed. 'How, though, can you know this? I mean, I can understand broadly, the idea, but how do you know it isn't indicating, say, *Strype*'s location?'

The Teapot Man thrust the sphere close to Mr Pixum's nose, causing him to back away.

'Look within,' he said, impatiently, as Mr Pixum merely frowned. 'Look! What do you see inside?'

Mr Pixum's eye roved about the network of rustic fibres, silver stars, some tiny red lights he hadn't noticed previously – perhaps they were obscured by the brighter light of the globes?

'Oh,' he said, 'Looks like a snuff box.' He glanced at his companion, his frown disappearing as realisation dawned. 'A personal possession. Sir Roger's psychic scent?'

'Just so,' replied The Teapot Man. 'I took the liberty of borrowing it from his study for such an eventuality.'

'Remarkable,' Mr Pixum repeated and went on to say, 'I con—'

There was a ping and a snap as several roots and twigs sprang loose, one of which flicked the end of Mr Pixum's nose. The Teapot Man grappled with the sphere as its component parts continued to assert their independence. It was a losing battle.

'Pah!' he said as it fell in bits and pieces through his hands. He dropped to the ground and began to pick up the snuffbox, globes, stars and whatnot from amongst the dried leaves of the woodland floor.

'It served its purpose,' said Mr Pixum, rubbing his nose. 'Remarkable,' he said for a third time.

'Pah!' said The Teapot Man for a second time.

They set off in a west-southwesterly direction that, curiously, led them back to Woodfold Bower.

Beech trunks soared in the moonlight, their exposed roots resembling hands with twisted fingers thrusting into the loam.

Mr Pixum remarked casually, 'Like columns of an ancient temple.'

'The columns of an ancient temple,' said The Teapot Man pedantically, 'were most likely designed to resemble the trunks of trees.'

Entering an unfamiliar clearing, Mr Pixum noticed for the first time just how cold the night had become. Frost was in the air . . . and something else.

'Don't look now,' said The Teapot Man.

'She's here,' sighed Mr Pixum. 'These woods are . . . strange.'

Exactly how strange Mr Pixum thought the woods were is not recorded, but it is safe to assume that what happened next was a good deal more strange than the Mage of Westrum Powers had allowed for.

Mr Pixum and The Teapot Man were thrown to the ground and rolled back and forth as if by invisible hands. Mr Pixum could feel his limbs and torso being squeezed. It was a sensation of being picked up by giant pincers and pushed around. Each time they picked themselves up, they were flung sideways, pushed over backwards, dragged over the ground or plucked into the air and dropped. They both spotted the spectre of Sad Annie barely visible in the penumbral light at the edge of the clearing.

'It's her!' yelled The Teapot Man in the midst of yet another tumble, 'She's bending space!'

'Not half as bad . . .' said Mr Pixum as he was slammed against a tree, ' . . .when you know just what it is!'

'Run!' shouted The Teapot Man.

Mr Pixum could not even get to his feet before he was thrown back to the ground, never mind run. Something splintered. 'The Teapot Man!' he thought. He willed himself to look and what he saw almost brought a tear to his eye. His friend's ingenuity amazed him.

The Teapot Man was standing, which was a feat in itself, holding a pair of dead branches horizontally at arm's length. Fallen branches littered the woodland floor. The pinching of space quickly snapped them—and each time, The Teapot Man just as quickly held up another . . . and another. All the time he was backing away from Sad Annie. Mr Pixum was a lightning study when the need was pressing—or squeezing—and immediately began to imitate his friend.

The Teapot Man shouted above the sound of splintering branches,

'Move back! Move back!'

Wondering how long it would be before they ran out of sticks, Mr Pixum needed no encouragement to retreat. To his relief, the power of "invisible fingers" became noticeably weaker the farther away they were from Sad Annie.

'Limited range,' gasped The Teapot Man, wedging a branch into the unseen grasp, 'When I say "run," *run!*'

'Say it then!' shouted Mr Pixum.

'Run!' said The Teapot Man. And that is what they did.

Having at last paused for breath and taken stock of their surroundings, they realised that west-southwest had been the last thing on their minds in their desire to put distance between themselves and Sad Annie. In short, they were lost . . . but not completely: in their flight they had run downhill, which was the easiest and quickest method of escape, and now they heard the stream as it chuckled over pebbles. They would follow it until they came across a familiar landmark. They decided to head once again for Woodfold Bower, this time by a more circuitous route, hoping not to re-encounter the spectre.

Happy to abandon his studies only that morning, Mr Pixum now longed for his armchair by the fire and a book.

They soon found the familiar path and avoided it. Pushing uphill through a hazel thicket, something caught Mr Pixum's eye before becoming hidden by the bushes. He took a step backwards and looked again. It was the glint of metal. He motioned to The Teapot Man to proceed with caution. It just was not possible to approach silently: the ground here was covered with dry leaves and any number of brittle twigs ready to snap under the slightest pressure.

After a whispered conversation, they agreed a plan. They would close-in on who- or whatever it was from opposite sides: if they were going to get a hostile reception, they could not be pursued in two directions, assuming who or what they were approaching was indeed in the singular. It wasn't a perfect plan but it was the best they could come up with.

As he drew closer, Mr Pixum could hear someone singing, or mumbling, a song. The song had barely any tune to it, but words such as 'gold' and 'treasure' were audible. He was so close now that he could see The Teapot Man within ten yards' distance, his Teapot reflecting twinkles of moonlight. A bar of darkness resolved itself into a fallen tree. Just above it was the Helm of Gagnir complete with horns of Dragon's Claw. From beneath it came the tuneless singing.

The moment Mr Pixum had taken in this sight, his mind blazed with the implications. Where was Mr Fox? The moment after that, he froze to the spot.

The gleaming Helm rose up . . . and up, raised upon the head of Oberon Strype, who sprang to his feet with a roar, swinging a huge double-bladed axe at The Teapot Man. Amazingly, he looked larger than life. The sound of the blade as it cut the air was terrifying. A swan's wings, thought Mr Pixum absurdly, would make that sound if they were beating at one hundred miles an hour.

The Teapot Man! What had become of him?

The axe sliced through branches and bushes as it swept the place where he had last seen his friend. His friend had vanished. The axe now came for him. He was swept off his feet; the blade scythed a fine dust of velvet from the tip of his top hat.

The Teapot Man said, 'Get up! Now! Run!'

Mr Pixum ran, barely registering that his friend had just saved his life, knocking him down a mere gnat's whisker before the arc of the blade had . . .

They ran as fast as they could but it was no use. Strype was faster, hacking trees and bushes; everything fell before his blade. They could feel his roar vibrating through the ground beneath their feet. It was only a matter of seconds before the axe cleaved them in twain.

Mr Pixum found himself in a silent place; the rampaging Strype had vanished. He remembered . . . something. It was a dream-like memory—not a real dream or a recollection of something that had actually happened in his own past—of being able to make a certain kind of effort of will perhaps, that enabled him to leap into the air and then "scrabble" incrementally higher by means of a sort of levitation.

He saw himself ascending thirty, forty feet from the ground. It felt real. He felt as if he could actually do it if he could get into a certain state; attain a new fusion of mental and physical wellbeing that would unleash incredible vitality, clarity and *balance*. It was that feeling of being "in tune," of perfect harmony with the univi, healthy, suffused with the glow of true optimism and *knowing what to do*. It was *the knack*!

This was one of those moments of grace that would be captured forever deep within his soul. Crystals of frost glistened on the treetops, the woodland possessed of an unearthly beauty as they sailed above it. Yes, "they"! Mr Pixum was aware of The Teapot Man riding the airs of night beside him. He experienced ecstasy. He *was* ecstasy—and inside that encapsulation of all that is perfect in the World of Existence, he understood that he had always known this. Had since his birth—and *before* his birth— known he could fly.

The technique of flying, or at least taking off impressively in a manner that is, without question, more than a mere leap into the air, is the achievement of running upwards without the benefit of a solid slope or even a ladder—in fact, without even the security of a taut rope or chain. Everyone can do it but alas, very few feel confident and self-realised enough to attempt it. With practice, it is even possible to descend in a graceful and dignified fashion.

The Teapot Man waved. Mr Pixum waved back. His left boot skimmed a treetop, dislodging a shower of ice crystals and dead leaves. His right boot caught another branch. That hurt! His heart lurched. He was anxious. After all, it was a long way to the ground—he could see patches of it through the trees. Whack! Luckily it was a soft branch, thin and springy. The next branch was equally springy, if slightly more harsh on the shins. As was the next, and the next . . .

Above the woods the moon sailed full and bright. Trees, majestic as "columns of an ancient temple," rose towards it. Limbs arched in silhouette: the awkward angles of oak antlers and the smooth structures of ash and beech. So snug here, so soft. A rushing sound—his chest inflated. Leaves rustled around him. Sitting up, he could see he was in the middle of a hollow full of dry leaves. He shook himself. His top hat sat on his head as neatly as it ever had. There was The Teapot Man, ceramic headwear also in place and intact. They climbed to their feet, swaying slightly, brushed themselves off yet again and began to walk.

'Great Pan!' thought Mr Pixum, 'I believe we've been looked after.'

Adrenalin would only take him so far now. Fatigue was setting in. He must find the resources within himself to fight it.

'Come in,' said Lady Quarterhawse, 'I hope you are the bearer of good news?'

Her eyes fell upon the Helm and she smiled.

Mr Fox was less than happy at being forced to come all the way around to the front of Woodscott House and knock—he'd been to the study window only to find it closed, the ladder nowhere to be seen and the room in darkness.

He handed over the Helm. Even in a grumpy mood he was sensitive to the feelings of others and felt uncomfortable when he admitted that her husband was, at the time he left his companions, still missing. Lady Euphemia Quarterhawse continued to smile.

'I expect he'll turn up,' she said.

Understandably, Mr Pixum and The Teapot Man were feeling rather stirred by their recent experience. It wasn't every day one escaped certain death. Escaping from certain death and suddenly finding oneself flying through the air in ecstasy happened but rarely in the single lifetime of most mortals and, even in the strangely meandering and somehow elastic lifetime of the likes of these two Feathers of Fate, it was unusual.

As well as the recent events, Mr Pixum thought about the tantalising "vision" he'd experienced when he'd accidentally touched Oberon Strype's sleeve. Something was awry there . . . he just couldn't grasp it. He had told The Teapot Man about it, of course. His friend had been a good listener and seemed to understand far more than he himself did, almost as if he'd been "in" on it. Come to think of it, it was much more in The Teapot Man's line than his. Most of us are used to viewing the theatre of life from the auditorium; The Teapot Man frequently sees it from backstage. Sadly, The Teapot Man could only theorise a psychic leeching taking place, much in the manner of certain vampyres. Doggedly, they set off once more in the direction of Woodfold Bower.

They had reached a decrepit fence in the wood and stood by an old broken gate hinged to a rotting gatepost.

'I know that tree,' said The Teapot Man, indicating an oak of great girth standing at the foot of a slope a few yards away.

'Of course!' Mr Pixum said, 'This is the tree beneath which Strype keeps his valuables!'

Warily, they made their way towards it. There was a chill in the air that had nothing to do with frost. The Teapot Man gave Mr Pixum a "not *again*" look.

Sad Annie looked even more forlorn than usual, thought Mr Pixum, as she drifted forwards beyond the great oak. He wondered whether he had the energy to wedge any more sticks into the air. He thought not.

A sound came from behind the oak. It might have been a word although it could equally have been a groan. What of Mr Fox?

Had he fallen before the axe-wielding Anglo-Saxon? If not, Mr Pixum hoped Bertie had flung the wretched Helm at Strype and scarpered. Was it him behind the tree though, lying wounded?

The shade of Sad Annie was more interested in whoever was groaning than she was in him or The Teapot Man. What if it *was* Mr Fox? He stalked towards the tree and peered around it, only to receive another surprise. He watched as Sad Annie, the beautiful shade, helped Oberon Strype to his feet. His clothes were dishevelled and blood ran down the side of his face.

The two Feathers of Fate overheard Strype telling Sad Annie that he'd been knocked out.

'By these people?' she asked with a gesture towards Mr Pixum peering around the oak. So much for his skills of stealth and concealment.

'No,' said Strype, his voice wavering, 'It was someone else.'

'Who, then?' asked the ghost.

'It was . . . It looked like . . . I rather think . . . it was me.'

'You are mistaken,' said Sad Annie, 'You have had a blow to the head.'

'No, he wore my clothes . . . Had my face and hair . . . He wore the Helm . . .'

'Possibly not mistaken but certainly confused,' said Mr Pixum, stepping forward. The Teapot Man quickly joined him.

'This is very peculiar,' murmured Mr Pixum, as he observed himself observing Sad Annie (and some of the moonlit wood that was visible through her), who was observing him. She was lithe, graceful and transparent.

'Keep away from my brother,' she said.

'Your brother?' asked Mr Pixum with raised eyebrows, immediately turning to Oberon, 'You once had a sister? This is her ghost, Sad Annie?'

'Tactful,' said The Teapot Man in Pixum's ear.

Oberon Strype spoke up. 'I still have a sister,' he said, 'but she is not "Sad Annie."'

He appeared to have recovered somewhat. He smiled and sighed.

'Gentlemen, meet my half-sister, Miranda.'

Mr Pixum also indulged in a sigh.

'Much as I dislike to state the obvious,' he said, 'I have to say this is most curious.'

'Would it help if I explained a few things?' asked Oberon Strype.

Now it was Miranda's turn to sigh.

Strype began by telling them of his late father, Percival Strype. He was an adventurous gentleman, never content with day-to-day routines, whom the young Oberon rarely saw. Percival became a collector of exotic items, and to collect these, he had to travel. On his travels he met some interesting people. One such interesting person taught him the art of sorcery. Thus Percival Strype became a collector, traveller and sorcerer. He would be away for months at a time, eventually becoming a stranger to his family. It was on one of these collecting trips that he acquired the Helm of Gagnir.

Percival and his wife, Hazel, decided to try for another child, possibly because Hazel told him she became lonely during his prolonged absences. Hazel particularly wanted a daughter. Being an accomplished sorcerer, Percival decided to help Nature with her decision by performing a ritual to ensure his wife became pregnant with a girl-child. He may have done it only to please Hazel. Oberon was certain his father did not discuss his plan with his mother. Had he done so, his mother would have had nothing to do with it—or him. The ritual was flawed. Oberon, of course, learned all this from his mother.

During Percival's incantations, a chaotic spirit materialised and treated him to an agonising death. It then forced itself upon Hazel. The spirit used Hazel's life force to generate a daughter, using her womb as a gateway for the girl to materialise. As she developed, so her mother weakened. It was not a full-term pregnancy: the ethereal girl emerged fully formed after only one month. It was not a birth in the normal sense, as can be imagined, but an *extrusion* of Hazel's essence fused with the essence of the anonymous spirit. The act of "giving birth" took the last of Hazel's vitality and she drifted into her final sleep shortly after entrusting Oberon with the care of his new half-sister.

It was Oberon's presence that saved Miranda from also fading away: she required a constant supply of life force to remain "alive." Oberon and Miranda had learned, from time and experience, that Miranda could thrive on no life force other than that given by her own kin, which meant, of course, that of her half-brother, as there were no other surviving relatives.

Miranda, Oberon explained, was a "kinetic spirit," a semi-wraith, who could partially appear and interact with the world, so long as she had a steady trickle of Oberon's vital force.

'Aha!' said Mr Pixum, as Oberon's words percolated into his mind, 'That was the message of my "vision" after I touched your coat. By what means I know not, I became conscious of the hole in your life force, depleted as Miranda constantly draws it off for her own needs. But I sensed your vital energy had a fresh quality about it all the same. Possibly because it always has to renew itself.' He shivered. 'The rest of the vision? Merely unnecessary revelations.'

Oberon had schooled Miranda in the world in which she found herself, helped her to accept her unique situation and to be happy. Oberon had explained to his half-sister that it would be wise, for obvious reasons, to keep her existence hidden from the outside world. She agreed. They lived in the family home, Woodfold Bower, in the woods, content in each other's company. Against the odds, they had come to terms with the past, put it behind them and lived for the present. They both understood that when Oberon died, Miranda would also cease to exist—at least as a "kinetic" spirit.

The legend of "Sad Annie," concluded Oberon, started with sightings of Miranda strolling in the woods. Nothing more than that.

When Strype began his story, The Teapot Man had kindled a small fire against the cold. It was now a healthy blaze.

'It feels strange after all this time. I was reluctant to venture out this night because I did not want you to meet Miranda. Now the two of you are the first people to share our secret.' He rubbed dried blood from beneath his eye. 'I don't know... I think it's a good thing to share it with others . . . At least with those we can trust.'

'You can rely on our discretion,' said Mr Pixum, 'Although much still depends upon the fate of Sir Roger and the missing Helm.'

Miranda said, 'And I apologise for assaulting you. I thought I was protecting Oberon.'

Mr Pixum sat on the skirts of his coat, wrapped in his thoughts. He mulled over all the facts and surmises and assumptions from every angle and no matter how many times he thought through it all, he always reached the same conclusion.

There was a cracking of twigs from the foot of the slope. Instantly alert, Mr Pixum, The Teapot Man and Oberon Strype rounded the oak and descended towards the source of the sound.

By the broken gate stood Euphemia Quarterhawse. With her hair now braided and wearing a black cloak about her shoulders, she resembled an Anglo-Saxon princess. The Helm of Gagnir, now compleat with Dragon's Claw horns, was upon her head. She was pointing a blunderbuss at them, and, Mr Pixum saw, there was a brace of pistols tucked into her belt.

Her eyes glittered though her face wore a calm expression. There would, thought Mr Pixum, be no reasoning with this woman. He could not allow it to end in this way. He had been too slow. If only he'd worked it out a few minutes sooner . . . As he cast his eye over the scene, looking for an idea, a means of escape . . . anything, he caught sight of the double-bladed axe almost covered with fallen leaves, lying a couple of feet from the gatepost. And in the sky he saw a red glow in the direction of Woodscott House.

Mr Fox awoke with a sore head and coughed. When he tried to move he found he was bound. Tied to one of the oaken newel posts at the foot of the great staircase. His feet and hands were bound tightly and a rope had been wound about his middle and lashed to the post. It was if he were being burned at the stake. A smashed pitch-jar lay on the flagstones amid a fury of flames. Broken oil lamps were scattered everywhere he looked. Tapestries were ablaze, curtains too. He noticed a longcase clock by the study door, although it was clearly recognisable as a Benjamin Lockwood there was something odd about its lines, its *stance*, how it looked strangely like a soldier standing guard . . .

The oak panelling had caught and, oh, Great Pan, flames were licking up the staircase where it turned at the first landing and were spreading in both directions: towards the ceiling and upper floors and down the stairs and banisters towards him.

'Stop,' demanded Lady Quarterhawse, 'You'll do very well just where you are.'

'You appear to have found the Helm,' said Mr Pixum, hoping this woman couldn't hear the pounding of his heart. Any show of fear would only awaken her cruel side, he thought. Then he mentally shook himself, thinking, Who am I kidding? Her cruel side never sleeps.

'And so you are of no more use to me.'

'We've been trying to help you,' he said, 'If it wasn't for my friend here,' indicating The Teapot Man, 'you would still be an occasional table. What is going on?'

'Between you, me and the gatepost,' said Lady Quarterhawse, 'Our plan worked a treat. A cunning imposture. Until you and your friends turned up, Pixum.'

She scowled. 'Took you long enough to arrive! My back is stiffened.'

'But what was the purpose of your "cunning imposture"?' asked Mr Pixum, 'What can you gain from it apart from an Anglo-Saxon artefact?'

'It won't hurt to enlighten you,' she said, 'Where you're about to go, I doubt there's much currency in idle gossip.'

Mr Pixum thought, Take your time. Armed to the teeth you can say anything you like, you arrogant gnashgabber. Standing there in that . . . cow helmet. He waited, said nothing.

'It was my stupid husband,' she said, 'Frittered away his fortune gambling and whoring, details he neglected to mention until after I married him. All I stand to inherit are his debts!'

She gave the old gate a vicious kick. 'Is that any way to treat a lady? As if I would have married that useless sponge for any other reason than his wealth!'

'So you knocked me out,' said Oberon, 'and blamed me for stealing my own Helm. Well, now you can find your own fortune.'

'Knocked you out?'

A look of puzzlement momentarily passed across her face. Then she shrugged.

'Wasn't me. It was obviously Sir Roger. A practicing sorcerer. When he told me, I thought, "Oh joy! We will be fabulously wealthy!" Useless. I should have guessed. That's his only trick, shift-shaping or how you say it.' A German accent was fighting to reinstate itself.

She aimed another kick at the gate but, weakened by her previous abuse, it chose that moment to collapse.

'We planned to disappear from inside a locked room, each of us would become an inanimate object. No one would suspect that. We would simply have vanished. When the search spread further afield we would make our escape.'

'We didn't find Sir Roger,' said Mr Pixum, 'Was he changed into an inanimate object when we discovered you?'

'The door to the study of course was him! We removed the real door and in the walled garden placed it.'

'Why now? What did you plan to do once you left Woodscott?'

asked Mr Pixum.

'We would put the blame on Strype, steal the Helm and find a new fortune. Or rather *I* would find a new fortune. I intended to do away with my pathetic husband . . . only now he is out there somewhere no doubt tying up loose ends—or he has deceived me, to leave me as a piece of casual furniture. No matter, I will see to him when I find him.'

She frowned as if at an unpleasant recollection. Collecting herself, she hefted the gun upwards, for its weight had tired her arm and it was pointing downward.

'We had to disappear before my husband's creditors came for us. It would have caused a scandal and ruined our reputations. Otherwise it would be the debtor's prison for us. The scandal could come out after we were gone. What would it matter then? We would reappear under new identities eventually.'

'You knew I had the Helm all along,' said Strype, 'Why didn't you ask me for it?'

'Would you have given it to me?'

'No.'

'You have your answer then. Sir Roger hates you, anyway. He blames you for the death of his daughter, as you know. He's convinced you killed her! Whenever he might have seen reason, back to your guilt I took care to steer him.'

Good fellow, thought Mr Pixum, Keep her talking. He sidled up to the gatepost and casually leaned on it.

Oberon stared at this woman, Lady Quarterhawse, a woman he thought he knew at least somewhat, his expression a mixture of forbearance and contempt.

'Why did he blame me? I *didn't* kill her,' said Oberon.

The heat was drying out his eyes. His fur and his coat were smouldering.

'*Mon bel habillement!*' moaned Mr Fox. From high in the house came a dull roar, like thunder, as if the fire, gaining appetite as it spread throughout the rooms, shouted in its victory. With a crash, burning roof timbers collapsed into what was left of the staircase.

'He needed someone to blame,' continued Lady Quarterhawse, 'You were in the right place. I didn't want him looking any deeper into it than was necessary.'

Oberon said, 'What was your motive? I mean, why . . ?'

'It was convenient. For me. I hated the spoiled *bitch*! At first sight she hated me. Feelings were mutual. It was her or me. I also killed the other two in the woods close to your house to throw on you the blame. I heard the "Sad Annie" story and encouraged it, feeding the rumour. It became very popular with the locals. I knew it would come back to you. Now you can take the blame for this, too.'

She swung the gun towards Mr Pixum . . . but instead of firing, she gasped.

'Sir Roger!'

The gatepost was changing into Sir Roger Quarterhawse. The metamorphosis dislodged Mr Pixum's elbow and he fell to the ground.

The look in Sir Roger's eyes was enough to tell Euphemia that he'd overheard everything she'd said.

Without hesitation, she fired. The gunshot echoed away among the trees leaving a shower of smoke and sparks swirling in the night air.

Mr Pixum made a lunge for the axe.

She saw him through the smoke. 'Stay!'

Mr Pixum stayed.

'Good dog.' She was clearly enjoying herself. '"Strype Strikes Again! Sensational Murder of Sir Roger and Two Underlings!" I can see the headlines now.'

'Wait!' said Mr Pixum, 'You are forgetting something!'

'I do not think I am,' said Lady Quarterhawse with a smile as cold as an Arctic blizzard. She threw down the blunderbuss and drew a pistol from her waistband.

'Yes, you are. Our friend Mr Fox will not rest until you are caught!'

'Oh, him,' she said, 'The other headline, my mind it almost slipped: "Fox Burglar *Crisped* In House Fire." Anything else I *forgot?*'

The hitherto silent Teapot Man spoke up.

'I think "forgot" is inaccurate, Lady Quarterhawse; possibly "were not expecting" fits better.' His arm swept gracefully out as if welcoming a guest.

Miranda, who had remained hidden behind some trees throughout the exchange, had now drifted into view, gliding across a carpet of dead leaves.

She was approaching Lady Quarterhawse whose eyes widened in disbelief.

'What? You're not real!' With a glance at Mr Pixum, she said, 'One of your tricks is this?'

Mr Pixum's voice was heavy with warning.

'She is not one of my tricks, I assure you.'

She raised the weapon. 'Stay back! Stay back or I'll shoot!'

Miranda continued to advance upon her.

When Miranda was six feet away from her, Lady Quarterhawse fired the pistol . There was another explosion, a fury of sparks and smoke was all that was visible where Miranda's head had been a split-second ago.

As the air cleared, Miranda, not a hair out of place, continued towards Lady Quarterhawse.

Stopping directly in front of her, Miranda punched her in the mouth with such force that Lady Quarterhawse's feet left the ground. Her head snapped back. They all heard the crack of bone. There was a simultaneous outrush of breath from Oberon. The Helm bounced into a hazel bush.

Mr Pixum looked at Sir Roger's body. What remained of his

head was thrown back, along with his upper torso, while the lower part was yet a gatepost, death having occurred before the change was completed.

'Zeus knows what the coroner will make of *that*,' he thought.

Oberon was at his sister's side.

'Are you hurt, sis?'

'Not any more, Obie. For the first time in years one thing I am not, is hurt.'

Her voice, now that Mr Pixum focused his attention upon it, was musical, like a woodland stream tinkling over a bed of pebbles . . .

Miranda embraced her half-brother. Oberon staggered. 'I need to sit awhile,' he said, 'The energy you used in that blow has left me decidedly drained.'

He sank to the bed of leaves, then, with a grin, said, 'Nothing some good roast beef won't restore.'

'Then it was Sir Roger who threw a grenado shell at us when we came up from beneath the tree,' said Mr Pixum, 'No doubt it was an attempt to take the Helm. We looked all about for you, Oberon, but you were nowhere to be seen. What happened to you?'

It was Miranda who replied.

'Oberon was stunned. I dragged him into a hollow and covered him with leaves. It was all I could do with the energy I had left. While my brother was unconscious I was unable to do anything but fade until he came to.'

The Teapot Man looked at Mr Pixum and answered the unspoken question on his friend's lips.

'Yes,' he said, 'I do remember how to fly.'

Mr Pixum snatched up the axe.

'My coat!' wailed the fox, gesturing with both hands, 'Look at my raggedy coat! And see my boots – they're cracked. Finest Spanish leather, ruined.'

The Teapot Man's eyes met the singular orb of Mr Pixum and

all three rolled skywards in a tribute to their mutual long-suffering. They both knew that Bertie Fox would easily replace these clothes from his extensive wardrobe, which consisted of several more identical outfits. Despite his lamentations, he wore his charred hunting apparel with more dignity than should have been possible, given its sorry condition.

By the light of the dying embers of Woodscott Hall, Mr Pixum looked at his own coat, herringbone tweed, now blackened and burned into holes on both sleeves. He saw The Teapot Man's coat had not escaped fire damage either. They would both have to resort to their respective tailors.

'Time we retrieved the chaise,' he said, 'Old Archie will be ready for a bag of oats. Speaking of sustenance . . .'

They walked away from the ruin, the rest of the world crisp with frost.

If anything could put Mr Fox out of his usual humour, his friends knew, it was an assault upon his fine attire. It was now evident that this rancour extended to the application of any combustive element to, or near enough to, his esteemed person. Fast and thick were his pantings.

'My whiskers! My fur!'

'Poor old Bertie,' said The Teapot Man, 'It's comforting to know that at least *some* folk are happy now.'

'But you don't understand,' insisted the fox.

'I agree,' said Mr Pixum, 'Now that the abscesses that were the Quarterhawses are well and truly lanced, the name of Strype is cleared of any smirch. Oberon and Miranda are once more free to live their lives in peace and contentment. Should they find any treasure by use of the Helm, they intend to donate their share to a charitable cause.'

'... I simply *cannot* appear in Society until my whiskers and my fur have grown back!'

'We'll never know,' said The Teapot Man.

'Never know what?' asked Mr Pixum.

'Of the people and objects we've encountered in these past hours, how many of them were truly themselves and how many were Quarterhawse in an altered shape, or even *other* things or people altered *by* him.'

'We could investigate,' said Mr Pixum, 'but the effort would outweigh its worth.'

'I agree. It's irrelevant now,' said Mr Fox, 'Prominent in my mind is refreshment followed by a feather bed. Our landlady will be eager for an explanation of the night's events; she can't have failed to see Woodscott burning.'

'On the contrary,' said Mr Pixum, plainly referring to the second of Mr Fox's remarks. 'It has taught us a valuable lesson.'

Mr Fox said, 'Appearances can be deceptive?'

'Just so, Bertie.'

'We already knew that.'

'So we thought. Yet we were taken in all the same.'

'We allowed ourselves to be deceived,' said Mr Pixum, 'We took things at face value because of the surroundings in which they were framed—and because of our inclination to believe that virago, it suited us to believe our eyes.'

'You mustn't be so hard on ourselves,' grinned The Teapot Man, 'All things are real in one sense or other, but not all things are true.'

'All depends upon what you mean by "real," ' said Mr Pixum, 'or "true." '

'The fire was real enough,' said Mr Fox.

'True,' said Mr Pixum.

With that philosophical enigma hanging in the air, they entered the lane and there was Archie at his tether. He seemed to be sleeping.

A few minutes later, as they were rattling along the road, Mr Pixum became aware of a figure making its way along the roadside; as they drew closer, he recognised the somewhat ungainly shape as Throtespear.

'Good day to you!' called Mr Pixum.

Throtespear nodded his greeting and held up a hand indicating they should halt the chaise.

'Busy night by all accounts, gentlemen,' he said, 'Terrible thing, the fire.'

He seemed to think about something, deciding whether to mention it.

'What is it?' asked Mr Pixum, 'Much has happened since we left the inn, anything you have to say is of interest to us.'

'Well, if you say so . . . It was . . . I was just . . . taking a stroll for the night air, you might say, and I saw Sir Roger Quarterhawse carryin' a great axe. I hid behind a tree, like, watching him. I thought, "What's he a-doing with that?" There's no need for 'im to chop his own firewood, I'm sure. Well, then I sees him come over all shimmerin' and sort of wrigglin' and next thing I sees is he's lookin' just like Mr Strype an' he's wearing a hold helmet. It staggered me, d'you know? Never seed the like, hever.'

'This—' began Mr Pixum.

'That explains the axe-wielding warrior,' The Teapot Man said, talking over Mr Pixum, 'Sir Roger had changed himself into Oberon Strype!'

'I was about to say,' said Mr Pixum, 'This confirms what I guessed at the time, or shortly after. Sir Roger wanted to annihilate the witnesses, everyone involved, in fact, and he would do his best to lay the blame upon Strype. Of course he wasn't going to murder Strype, he needed him alive so that he could be caught and executed, therefore putting the whole matter to rest. It's certain no one would believe anything Strype said, his reputation had already been sullied by the Quarterhawses.'

'Is that so?' The Teapot Man asked rhetorically, 'Because to me it bears the stamp of "deduction by hindsight."'

'We are grateful, Mr Throtespear,' said Mr Pixum, ignoring his friend's remark, 'for helping us tie-up the last loose end in this tale of knavery.'

'Be that as it may, good sirs, I'll be heading to my cot, this bout's bin altogether wearisome.' He hoisted a sack over his shoulder and trundled off along the lane as Mr Pixum shook the reins, 'Go on, Archie!' he said.

There was a blush on the horizon directly ahead, in the direction of Scopwick Green, a rose tint merging into robin's egg blue. A fresh day, sharp and smelling of . . .

'Toast!' said Mr Fox, his nose a wonder when it came to things epicurean, 'F. Bagnell, innkeeper, has breakfast on the go!'

*Alas, the occasion of Sonny Tiphareth's manifestation to the three friends is for another time.

The Walking Tour

'Westrum Powers is situated to the west of East Westerham. No one knows whether "Westrum" is a corruption of "Westerham" or whether "Westerham" is a corruption of "Westrum," all lost in the mists of . . . thingummy,' explained Mr Pixum, clearly unwilling to go over the history of his homestead to assuage the idle curiosity of the, well... idle, yet again, but doing so nonetheless.

'There's been a settlement here for over two thousand years. Trouble is, it seems to have meandered around the general area over time, beginning *here* and then abandoned, rising up *there* or nearby and then abandoned again, cropping up back where it probably began or a mile or so away—even producing several outcroppings at once, which, I suppose, is how there came to be a Westerham and an East Westerham—and a South Westerham. There was an even a West Westerham although the Pixums lay claim to that spot, which is here, where the Pixum family pile stands on top of an earlier Pixum family pile.'

'What of the *other* name?'

'Oh, "mists of time" again, old chap. Ought to be the family motto, eh?'

'Surely there must at least be a few suppositions?'

Mr Pixum had been stirring wayside grasses with the end of his stick but now, without warning, he violently bashed the fence with it. This act of madness or brutality; Mr Pixum wasn't sure how his interlocutor perceived it, was simply frustration. He wanted to be *off*; to be *going*. When residing at his country house he loved to step into the dawn and through the dewy meadow, this was something for which he yearned when in London. He was determined that his early start would not be delayed any longer than he could help: he *would* gather enough mushrooms for breakfast! But instead of sending this person on his way, he merely forced a grin.

'Fenceworm,' he replied absently. He had, in fact, surprised himself. "Fenceworm" indeed! The words were out now however, despite being meaningless and worse, untrue. Ah well, there was now no going back; the fiction would have to stand on its own feet.

'*Fenceworm?*'

'It's nothing. Gets everywhere. Have to show 'em who's in charge.'

And to show his companion he meant business, he proceeded to thrash the fence with a savagery quite unbecoming, though in truth this was only an act intended to disguise his original lapse, all the time knowing he was doing no more than making it worse. Presently, he desisted.

'Er, the name? You were saying?'

Confound the man. Best get it over with.

'To be absolutely vague with you, I shall continue to hold up the "mists of time" shield. Antiquity has a lot to answer for, particularly with regard to historians, don't you think?'

Without allowing an answer, he continued.

'Yes, there *are* several theories as to what could be the origin of the name "Powers," but as yet there is no hard evidence for any of them. "Powys" is one possibility, pointing to a possible Cymric connection—indeed there *was* a Cadwallader Eagle Pixum, so you can see how that might draw some votes, particularly from the Welsh. Another popular candidate is "Powders"—a little more difficult to justify as it seems unlikely, whatever it means, that it would have been used as part of a name for the Pixum family seat.'

Accepting there would be no escape from this incorrigible

trivia sponge, Mr Pixum threw down his stick and basket and rummaged in his pockets for pipe and tobacco, finally giving himself up to the moment.

'There *is* a tenuous, though slim, chance for "Powders" too. Shake the family tree and out falls one Roderick Telemachus Bucephalus Pixum, a renowned alchemist. Alchemy, incidentally, is something practiced for centuries by most of the male line of the Pixums. Perhaps Roderick was known as "Powders" Pixum and dispensed his "philosopher's stone" from Westrum? The philosopher's stone has many forms, one such is a red powder . . .'

Taking up his stick once more, he attempted to bat a falling leaf with it and missed. A sudden thought came into his head that if only old Bertie Fox were here he could take this hapless passer-by on a tour of the local watering holes and he would probably *enjoy* it, by Lugh, knowing him. But Bertie already had a similar job to do, as and when their visitor arrived.

Where are you Mr Fox? he almost spoke the words aloud, Come and relieve me of this oaf!

He resumed.

'There are several other contenders, none of them worth wasting time on. "Powell," "Towers," "Watchtower"—now *that's* one I quite favour; there could well have been a Saxon watchtower on the spot. "Bowers," "Flowers"—there could be something in these two too, so to speak, for the park and formal gardens are, or rather were, sublime, landscaped by none other than Culpability Brown. But endearing as that is, it is as equally unlikely as the others. The current house, incidentally, was designed by William Winde . . .'

Mr Pixum was gabbling.

' . . .and built by my great great grandfather, Culpepper John Pixum, who fell for another of Winde's houses in Lincolnshire and commissioned him to design something similar, which is what we see today, although the observatory was added by my grandfather, the astronomer, Trelawney Eagle "Eagle Eye" Pixum. As I said, it's all conjecture, nothing proven, possibly ultimately unimportant—but then, who knows? What's in a name? Discovering the truth could well turn out to be crucial for all we know.'

The stranger mumbled something.

'Balls? Balls did you say?' Mr Pixum wasn't at all sure.

Visibly annoyed, the stranger cleared his throat and replied with no patience whatsoever, 'That's what I said. Billiard balls!'

He collected himself. 'Is there a fives court or a cricket pitch at Westrum by any chance? A billiard table perhaps?'

Damn the fellow! Odd question. Was he now trying for an even more banal line of trivia?

Mr Pixum knew he would never make a good batsman as he regarded all bally-sticky games as a waste of time. As for Mr Fox, his notion of "sport" held a different meaning entirely and The Teapot Man had the univi to analyse and synthesise without becoming distracted by these absurd follies. Another thought: I have no objection to follies as long as they are my idea. Why, I delight in absurdity as a means of navigating the labyrinth of so-called "reality," the essential quixotic and profound mysteries of existence . . . and the capricious if not malicious behaviour of seemingly inanimate objects.

Mr Pixum heard a rustle in the trees. Their heads turned in its direction.

Mr Fox appeared behind them. Heads swivelled back.

'Ah, Mr Fox, this is Mr ah . . . from Shaftesbury or Shropshire or somewhere, sightseeing you see? Knapsack and all? He's indulging his passion for architecture and other items of interest, savouring noteworthy specimens. As there are some lovely inns in the vicinity, I wonder whether you'd care to . . .'

'*Certainment. Nous allons* right away old fellow! Top you up?' Mr Fox's smile metamorphosed into his slyboots grin.

Visibly intimidated, the "hapless passer-by" nevertheless plucked up the courage to ask a question. Mr Pixum realised his companion had been wearing a look of frustration for some time that he hadn't taken the trouble to acknowledge.

'But what about the *other* name?' Peevish tone, brave soul.

'For Heimdall's sake, *what* other name?' asked Mr Pixum, fried mushrooms now plentiful in his field of vision. Breakfast Ho!

'Why, Fallingham Hall, of course!'

Mr Pixum, the penny dropped at last, had somehow melted away into a stand of beeches beyond which a dew-bejewelled meadow glistened in beams of morning sunshine. Mr Fox caught the telluric bouquet of field mushrooms wafting on the last wisps of mist . . .

Placing a guiding arm around the stranger's shoulders, Mr Fox steered him back into the lane. He said, his voice a purr yet with a definite undercurrent of chiding,

'You have strayed, my friend. Presently I will put you on the path leading to your true destination. Meanwhile . . .'

'I don't want . . .'

'No trouble at all,' assured the fox brightly, giving the man a sideways glance, a gleam in his yellow eyes. 'Step lively! *Maintenant!* A brisk stroll will take us to our first port of call—The Golden Fleece! An excellent hostelry! The roast beef and the ale I can heartily recommend! The sun will be well over the yardarm by the time we arrive!'

'B-but I insist ins—'

'Very kind of you, *mon ami.* Do I accept your offer of refreshment? *Mais oui!* Once fortified, we shall visit several other establishments in which you can continue to express your gratitude. And, solely for *your* gratification, I will continue to expound upon their architectural merit, history, legend and whatnot—all in abstruse hermeneutical tropes and, *comme il faut,* discuss the finest ales in empirical fashion!'

It was mid-morning by the time Mr Fox and the somewhat unwilling stranger crossed the threshold of their first hostelry, The Golden Fleece, which was situated in the middle of a hamlet of cottages that to Bertie Fox seemed at once harsh and somewhat hilarious—the promise of fine ale always induced a desire to view things with a smirk of a decidedly mordant quality.

The Teapot Man had travelled to London from East Anglia, inspected the home of the late Mr Skeem Falthoe and returned to East Anglia from London, all in order to more clearly understand just why those thrums in the Webs of Fate quivered in such a tenebrous manner. Now he had more than a good idea: he had completed the picture . . . and he knew it was time to act.

As Mr Fox passed through the dimly-lit hall of hornbeam panelling that had been smoothed by a hundred years of tipsy shoulders, a hand slipped out from a shadowed recess and pressed a note into his hand. This was done so sneakily that Mr Fox, having seconds before drained his fifth mug in this, the fifth inn of his improvised walking tour, slipped it into the pocket of his waistcoat and surprise made no appearance at this occurrence, which was surprising in itself. This visit had been dispiriting and he was glad to step outside. At this point, reflected the fox, I could simply forget about the note, which would instigate all manner of repercussions . . . but I won't, I will read it the very next time my companion takes to the bushes to relieve himself. Ah, there he goes now . . .

The landlord of The Solemn Cat, one Firdaws Khan, had held forth about his collection of small pebbles, all with a bluish hue, that he had placed upon his scales and only selected those that weighed two ounces exactly.

'The wee stones must always begin with an "O" and placed to the left—but only if the moon is waxing, in all other phases it must be placed just to the right of the middle,' said Khan in a voice that both rumbled and lilted. He was built like a stack of bull mastiffs, balanced a green smoking cap on a head the size of a pumpkin and his whiskers appeared to be attempting to leave his jowls in various horizontal directions. He continued to waffle.

'To the left or just right of the middle of what?' he asked

rhetorically and went on, 'I always find myself at this point, unable to formulate an answer and the situation at this moment has not changed for decades, but even so, there are tendrils attached—blue and tapering—but attached to what?'

Mr Fox noticed that now, with a finger, Khan seemed to be attempting to prize something out of the molars in his lower left jaw. Lower left jaw? Well, there is no *upper* jaw. *Alors!* Khan is off again . . .

'Though I wath only half-aware of carrying out thith tathk,' said the landlord, the finger rooting around in his mouth with admirable fixity of purpose, 'I recognithe the feeling of inthight it generathe in what theemth to be an appropriate corner of my mind and thuth I feel uplifted—'

This fascinated Mr Fox not one jot. Unfortunately his "accompaniment," this most irksome of strangers, was listening as if his life depended upon every syllable. Just as the fox was about to say, 'Drain your flagon, we'll be on our way,' his new "friend" butted in.

'An exciting life you lead my dear man! Placement of stones! Insight from dental debris! Quite extraordinary!'

The fox stood by, appalled, wondering how long before he deserted his mission. He noticed the five other customers of this establishment had somehow managed to squeeze themselves into the corner of the tap room farthest away from Khan and his soliloquy.

The stranger resumed. 'You will find it interesting to know that I too lead a colourful life. I often become a butterfly.'

Setting down his drink he crossed his hands at the wrists and flapped them slowly, presumably in imitation of the aforementioned insect. 'I then feed off a fat old toad until I have had enough and off I flit in search of another one.' He giggled. 'When I find a new toad I fill my belly and once again become a butterfly!' He reprised his "butterfly" hands. He looked very pleased with himself. Khan's face resembled a heap of his own stones.

On top of this, the companion having become even more

arrogant and annoying, 'Of course, as a fox I don't expect you to understand,' 'Wag your tail, swat these corpse flies away from me, there's a good chappie!', Mr Fox knew several more hours in his company remained. *I have heard a horse's arse speak with more eloquence and a good deal more sense*, he thought. In sum, all this was enough to make anyone at least partially browned off. In spite of this, the insouciant fox remained, on the surface, unruffled and as urbane as ever, relishing his ale and comestibles, the sparkle in his eye undiminished.

The fox took out the note and read it. It was from Mr Pixum reminding him of the already-agreed-upon place, more or less, but more importantly it gave him what he'd been waiting for: a time. Even with this latest crumb to add to the two crumbs Pixum had previously shared with him—what to do with this man, a place and now a time—to have any idea of the direction in which this escapade was heading he was in dire need of a decent fingerpost, though he sensed that was not to be. He would understand when it was time to understand. The stranger lurched from the bushes buttoning his breeches. The oaf returns, thought Mr Fox with a sigh.

Mr Pixum had had the dog-cart made ready. The Teapot Man, recently arrived at Westrum Powers and in need of sustenance after two days aboard coaches and the rigours of flea-infested truckle beds, had been fed and watered. Mr Pixum tightened the reins as The Teapot Man swung up beside him.

Mr Fox and his companion, who had become increasingly vinegary inn by inn, a condition that had had no effect upon the fox's ability to prevent his colleague's generosity from flagging, for he had indeed stumped up for each mug of ale, pie and crumbling cheese the pair had consumed thus far, sometimes without complaint—and whom Mr Fox now knew laboured under the following epithetical series: Mr Vinal Mabeus Haze Bentley—had now arrived at their seventh and, in all probability, last destination, The Last Edict Inn.

At the beginning of this ludicrous "tour" Bertie Fox had forced himself to deliver his promise, with well-feigned enthusiasm, to expound upon the "architectural merit, history, legend and whatnot" of the various establishments they fell into upon their way, but the "abstruse hermeneutical tropes" had been a promise too far, they had dried up after the first refreshment stop. After treating this wayfarer to such fascinating gems as 'The Old Bell is over six hundred years old, built from the ruins of a redundant lighthouse and was once converted into a life-sized doll's house by Lord— who never grew up and suffered from abysmally poor eyesight. He was heartbroken when his wife, Lady—, took up residence here, preferring the company of the dolls to that of her husband and his family,' and 'The Fogmonger's Gloves was originally called The Frogmaker's Thumbs, famous for it's ale and sewing repairs. Two hundred years ago it was taken over by one Charles Dual, a frogmaker from Woodbridge, and the business thrived until he and Mistress Dual drifted apart, whereupon he vanished overnight and the holding stood empty for fifty years. His ghost has appeared regularly over the decades, disturbing travellers in the night by darning their hose while they lay a-bed. You will observe the inn to be an outstanding example of the vernacular style,' and having to put up with a number of sots and taproom bores, as well as playing host to his tedious guest, these commentaries, most of which he invented as he spoke, were so obviously unappreciated and therefore redundant, that he gave them up.

Shadows had lengthened and autumnal chill had arisen in direct proportion to the sinking of the sun when Mr Fox said, 'Bentley, my fine fellow, pray step this way, there's something you need to see,' at the same time steering his associate away to the right of the old Edict, convivial establishment though it was. An impressive tower, round in shape, reared above an assembly of birch trees that glowed carmine and gold, russet and tangerine in their seasonal livery. The tower was built of limestone and red brick, its rounded column interspersed with arched windows placed seemingly at random in its walls, a conical roof of small red tiles crowned with a spherical golden finial topped it off. As they drew closer they could see derelict outbuildings assembled about its base. At the foot of the tower a short flight of stone steps led up to an arch that housed the doorway.

'Look inside,' said Mr Fox.

'Insignificance has my skin crawling; this edifice however, is certainly worthy of my attention,' said Bentley, 'I have had enough ale to last me a lifetime. This is surely the pinnacle of a most edifying diversion. Lead on, fellow.'

'The day is running away,' said the fox, gesturing Bentley ahead . . . and under his breath he murmured, 'though trickery is ever present.'

Mr Fox was about to follow Bentley up the steps when he became aware of a disturbance in some nearby hazel bushes. A squirrel wearing a tweed jacket and plus fours stepped out from behind the golden leaves.

'Good afternoon to you, Sir . . . Mr Fox, I presume?' he said, 'Dr Dilan Weston at your service . . . er, *was* at your service at The Solemn Cat.'

He winked, rubbed his fingers together. Mr Fox returned the wink briefly, dipped two white-gloved fingers into his pocket and spun a half-sovereign in the squirrel's direction. Dr Weston snatched it from the air, bit into it once, pocketed it, nodded his head three times, whispered,

'A small mercy is not enough,' and disappeared back into the hazel thicket.

Their footsteps raised echoes from the flagstones, resounding up into the crepuscular coils of a spiral staircase, ancient and crafted from oak, which curled upwards following the tower's round inner walls.

'There is something you need help with.' The voice was familiar to Bertie Fox but unfamiliar to Mr Bentley.

The Teapot Man stepped from behind a long case clock that stood to the left of the entrance. 'Lord Ferdinand Sleight of Fallingham Hall at your service. In your satchel you have a cylinder. You wish to have it opened as you cannot do it by yourself.'

The Teapot Man waited.

Bentley stared, his eyes showing shock and calculation. Eventually he said, 'How did you . . ?'

'Ways and means, Bentley, ways and means.' The Teapot Man smiled. 'Take out the cazexion.'

'The what?' said Bentley, clearly discomfited.

'The cylinder you wish to open. The cylinder bequeathed to you by your late friend, Mr Skeem Falthoe,' The Teapot Man held out his hand. 'I have the power to open it.'

Bentley opened his bag and slid out the cylinder. It resembled a section of birch branch with silver bark, on each end was a cap of brass in need of a polish. The Teapot Man grasped it and holding a hand over one end, muttered what sounded like '*Eldwit, eldwit, luzzen.*' He plucked at the end-cap and off it came. Immediately he handed back the cylinder to Bentley.

'Climb the stairs slowly and tell me what you see,' said The Teapot Man.

Taking hold of the rail, Bentley ascended the treads carefully, all the while staring into the cylinder. The staircase groaned beneath his weight, each step producing a creak of a different pitch.

Suddenly the sounds stopped.

'Ah! It's a . . . The cylinder . . .There's a beetle. It's crawled out into my hand!'

'Let it alone,' said The Teapot Man who turned to Mr Fox and whispered, 'Staphylinus, one of the roves, this one's a Staircase Beetle, *Ocypus carniface internuntio*, he is Lord Tertius Mantle QC. He's very fair.'

'The beetle, it's growing . . . Help me!' Bentley began to make moaning sounds. The staircase seemed to creak with renewed enthusiasm . 'I can't move!'

Creaks from the staircase, which had begun to writhe and judder, increased in volume, sharp bangs filled the tower with echoes.

'The Staircase Beetle is making his judgement,' said The Teapot Man, raising his voice above the noise, 'We should leave the tower now.'

The Teapot Man and Mr Fox descended the steps and found Mr Pixum awaiting them, his solemn expression lending his features a cadaverous cast.

'Trickery comes asking for bread,' he said, 'He is a stain upon nothingness.'

'How did this come about?' asked Mr Fox, 'I took him on the tour but the few hints I received merely raised more questions.' He looked from one to the other of his friends and stroked his whiskers with a gloved hand, the action somehow projecting naked and faintly offended curiosity.

An owl hooted from somewhere beyond the outbuildings.

Mr Pixum turned to The Teapot Man.

'Perhaps you would care to enlighten our friend?'

'Of course,' he said, 'It will be my pleasure.' He adjusted the teapot on his head and perched himself on a pile of ivy-covered masonry. 'First of all I felt some disturbing tremors along the Webs of Fate. Upon investigation, I narrowed them down to Deception and Trickery. The location was in London and it's there that I went and, after some diligent inquiring eventually arriving at the home of Mr Skeem Falthoe. He knew he hadn't much time left to him but wished to set in train a scheme to ensure he could expire knowing he would leave this world a satisfied man. We discussed the situation from all directions until eventually we arrived at a plan.'

'Why had I heard practically nothing of this until last night?' asked the fox, adding, 'And even that was very little.'

'You were busy with other things if I recall correctly,' said Mr Pixum, 'It was a kindness not to disturb you unnecessarily.'

Mr Fox looked suitably unabashed. He nodded his ingratitude.

The cracking sounds coming from the tower's doorway had grown deafening and were now accompanied by rumbling as of some infernal machinery at work.

The Teapot Man continued, almost shouting to be heard above the din.

'Falthoe's plight was this: he had been systematically robbed over a long period of time by his "friend," Mr Vinal Bentley to use his "country name" and whose "town name" is Vinnie Mabberly although Falthoe only knew him as Ella Dessai, a most convincing courtesan in her finery according to verifiable accounts, and who made quite an impression in London Society. Falthoe only discovered the thefts by accident when he took ill. He sent for his solicitor to amend his will, leaving his estate to Bentley—or Dessai. When they looked at the value of his estate they were shocked at how little remained. What Falthoe didn't know at the time was that Bentley had been feeding him poison by installments, as it were, anticipating just such a bequest. When the doctor discovered Falthoe's illness was due to poisoning it was already too late to save him.

'Now to our plan. The first thing Falthoe did was find a suitable beneficiary, in his case it was a home for retired cats, and then, at Mr P's advice (for I had corresponded with him during the planning stage), we introduced the "cazexion", a cylinder purported to contain the key to unimaginable wealth that could only be opened by means of a certain magical process, and this became Bentley's bequest. This was duly signed over to him. The next thing I did was to feed a rumour that there was a mage and a scholar in East Anglia, specifically at Fallingham Hall, a certain "Sir Ferdinand Sleight", the only magician in England with the particular experience to carry out such a task. We chose Fallingham as "Sleight"'s home because of its proximity to Westrum Powers and the real owner agreed to pass on to Poddy any communications from Bentley. Upon receipt of such a missive Mr P would invite Bentley to visit, give directions but subtly misdirect him by way of Westrum. Mr P also took care of the other details. Everything was in place, all we had to do was wait for Bentley to show u—'

From the tower came a scream so loud it ripped the very air to shreds.

Then a great silence stole the moment.

Then the creaking and cracking resumed.

'That will be Dame Ulyssa,' said The Teapot Man.

'Dame Ulyssa?' Mr Fox frowned, 'There was no one inside the Tower but us and Lord Mantle!'

'Dame Ulyssa is the spiral staircase,' said The Teapot Man with a smile, 'Dame Ulyssa Perkins . . . A wave crashing against a long shoreline wants the Truth . . . and so does she.'

Mr Fox, rubbing his eyes then scratching his head, muttered, 'Nice to know . . .'

The creaking sounds died slowly away.

'Lord Mantle and Dame Ulyssa work together within the Tower of Judgement,' said Mr Pixum, '"*Childe Roland*, or rather Vinal, *to the Dark Tower came*[1]". We stand at it's foot. Bentley was a murderer, a man of greed, a man without conscience, a man who thought only of himself. Dame Ulyssa Perkins and Lord Mantle have meted out Bentley's reward.'

Merde, thought Mr Fox, I have to know. 'He's been . . . er . . . executed?'

'So Bentley believes,' replied Mr Pixum.

Something else had been itching Mr Fox's mind.

'Why did the plan include today's walking tour?'

'Practicality,' Mr Pixum said, 'It was easy to have Bentley deliver himself to East Anglia: while he believed "Ferdinand Sleight" of Fallingham Hall could open the cazexion we knew he wasn't looking elsewhere for assistance and therefore we wouldn't lose him. The other reason was that you would enjoy a delightful epicurean treat and, to give him a taste of his own medicine: Bentley could pay for it.'

'"Enjoy" is not the word I would choose,' thought Mr Fox, though he replied, 'And you needed to keep him occupied until you knew when Dame Ulyssa would be available to consider his crimes. " . . .at dusk" said the note. After all, you couldn't expect Bentley to wait around all day. And Lord Mantle was inside the cazexion all the time, certainly for a number of days. Presumably he's a beetle of great patience?'

'Very,' replied Mr Pixum.

The three Feathers of Fate stood in silence and contemplated this consummation for a few minutes. Presently Mr Pixum spoke.

'Have a look inside would you, Bertie? Make sure all is in order.'

Mr Fox mounted the steps and disappeared into the tower.

'Been meaning to ask, mushrooms plentiful this morning, Poddy?' asked The Teapot Man, 'An enjoyable breakfast?'

'Ambrosial, Teep, ambrosial.' Mr Pixum rolled his eye and almost grinned.

Descending the steps at a skip, Mr Fox called out, 'All spic-and-span. No sign of the beetle . . . Lord Mantle. Staircase restored. The Dame sends her regards.'

As they strolled around to The Last Edict, the creaking of a nearby watermill could be heard. A cockerel crowed into the dusk.

'A fine evening,' said Mr Pixum, 'And I'm famished! Ready for supper, Bertie?'

'After all I've consumed today? A brandy will be sufficient to restore mind and body,' said Mr Fox.

'And for me, a pot pie and a pot of ginger tea will be tip-top,' said The Teapot Man.

That afternoon a stranger made his way along the drive towards Westrum Powers. After much traipsing about the locality he came to the conclusion that there was a mistake in his instructions. He limped along the drive, ascended the steps and knocked at the door, intending to ask for directions. After knocking several times he concluded the place was deserted, locked up. Well, he'd have to find his way to Fallingham Hall somehow and ask this

Ferdinand Sleight fellow if he would use his magical skills to retrieve his purloined effects. He had intended to arrive hours ago; he'd been not a mile down the road when a thief snatched his satchel. He knew the thief, that was what was so galling. At the time, lying in the roadside dust, he'd almost exploded with exasperation. Teddy Chorsque, the worst of the worst, the most devious killer and confidence-artist in London, must have caught wind of his quest and followed him.

1. *Childe Roland to the Dark Tower Came*, Robert Browning (1812–1889)

The Tale of The Tail of The Dark and the Head of the Tale of the Heart of The Light

For the seventh time Mr. Pixum peered through the murk in his parlour. The lamps were all lit. Even the multi-dimensional *Otz Chiim*, which usually provided enough reading light by itself, was barely visible within its cabinet. The clock had ticked away one hundred and twenty minutes since the sun, cold and red, had bled the last of the evening into the west, behind the black bristles of Hyde Park. An operculum of cloud had palled the last of the light, weeping chill tears upon the ubiquitous rooftops.

Anticipating a pleasant evening by the fire with Rimbaud and Goethe, Mr. Pixum placed upon the side table his volumes of choice. He stirred the smoking fire, but it declined to blaze and, like a vexed mistress, withheld its warmth. There was another thing: time was all wrong. Pockets of small duration were stretched or contracted inconveniently, while extended intervals yawned meaninglessly. Apathy sat upon Annoyance and stared into the middle distance.

'Ormuzd!' invoked Mr. Pixum, shaking himself, "Allow me enough radiance to read by, I beseech you!"

He supplemented the lamps with a host of candles but the room remained obstinately glim. The pointy-eared scholar sat himself down with a sigh, reached out a hand for one of his chosen books—but did not complete the action. A weariness arose within his breast; a flatness most uncharacteristic of this accomplished mystic. He sat motionless, contemplating this sinking feeling, analysing it, approaching it from various directions. He attempted to recoup his lost vitality, but after an hour of Taoist practises he felt little better. He opened his eye and stood.

'Perhaps I've lost my edge. Too much study and good living; not enough challenge.'

He looked out of the window.

'I feel lost,' he said.

He gazed over the lamp-lit windows, the naked branches, the glistening cobblestones. The street was empty. He could hear gurgling from the drainpipes, the moaning of the rain-wind as it slouched reluctantly along the bricks, doors, sills and sashes, compelled by its very nature to wander all of London's streets, squares, alleyways and parks. Mr. Pixum pressed his forehead to the cold pane. His nostrils were assailed by the aroma of the inside of windows: of wintry rain, of wind, of wild alien places of dark and light unfamiliarity, of street dust. This would, hitherto, have filled him with strange longings, of the promise of other places and other times. Now, though he could remember having had those sensations, he could no longer feel how he used to feel when inhaling window-grime. In fact, it became chillingly apparent, he could no longer feel anything at all. Resignedly he lit a pipe, a pipe that would not light. He poured a glass of port, took a sip of lamp oil; crumbled a piece from the Stilton; spat a mouthful of soil into the grate. A look of concern materialised upon his countenance—an expression, which, when worn upon this particular face, was the equivalent of a look of panic when worn upon any less extraordinary countenance.

Mrs. E had prepared his bath, but even this normally pleasant pastime now seemed utterly fatuous. Mr. Pixum, the renowned mystic and unhappy bather, remained immersed, tense and woeful, until, life being what it is, or rather, what it had just become, the water forced him out of his liquid misery by performing a thorough job of chilling his bones.

'This has gone far enough,' said the blighted one, snatching up his towel, 'Some country air, I think.'

He opened his carpet bag and began to pack.

'Put these in the post, please.'

He handed two letters to Mrs. Enderby, his housekeeper.

'Prepare yourself for a journey, Mrs. E.'

Mr. Pixum retired, thinking 'I really ought to sleep with my Magick Eye in my socket at a time like this, but a good, sound sleep is more easily to be had if I place it in its casket.'

And life being what it had become, the doom, which was being visited upon Mr. Pixum, arrived in its full majesty as Mystic and Eye unrested in their separate beds, so to speak.

The diminutive wearer of a teapot was peering at the scene that presented itself, circularly framed, beyond the barrel's opening. It had been a long day, comparing the patterns of grain (none alike) to be found inside the oak barrel, by the light of a single candle, with the pungent odour of its previous contents and with the sounds which the two things evoked in the mind of The Teapot Man (for it was he), the red teapot upon his head glinting in the candle's flickering but otherwise unremarkable flame.

Wood textures, adze-cuts, saw-cuts, staining—all threw some light upon the ponderable, defined cartouche of ideas assembled as a question-feeling-cognisance-satori maggot that writhed within The Teapot Man's unknowable mind, if "mind" is the appropriate word. Nomenclature aside, the light thus thrown was an infinitesimal point of an exceedingly large whole (only The Teapot Man will not call it "whole" because it never will be complete unless it all goes wrong). This was merely a part of one of The Teapot Man's infinitely complex yet blood-curdlingly simple but oblique studies. At that moment he would be fairly satisfied if he could realise the "is-ness" of the article while contemplating it against, amidst and apart from myriad connexions, tastes, scenes, concepts, theories, wheezes and fancies. He was disturbed in his interior meanderings when the outside world, as revealed by the barrel's open end, began to revolve in a clockwise direction. This was outrageous. The wrong kind of life *would* keep impinging upon his realisations.

'This is far from the first time I've been disturbed while on the cusp of an important node,' muttered The Teapot Man. The candle rolled over, died, carried on rolling. As did the barrel. As did The Teapot Man. Thus The Teapot Man, Tea-Mage and Feather of Fate, was visited by the doom while ferociously concentrating upon woodgrain.

The doom took its time with Mr. Fox, bon viveur, epicurean. It seeped slowly into his person, insinuating itself as he was sipping a morose brandy, collapsing his lustful thoughts about his ears like so many pavilions with their poles kicked away. He stared glassily into the darkest corner of the room, seeing only a different darkness within.

The inn clock ticked away its dingy seconds . . . Mr. Fox was the last to leave.

The last to leave by five hours.

The Chirp Inn of Pigwidgin Corner had long closed its doors for the night upon the merry band of wassailers, sailors, revellers and roisterers of unrefined habit.

The establishment was encumbered with an innkeeper who slept soundly in his cups for half the night and half the morning. He had such a wife, a vixen, who cleaved not unto her husband, but whose amply serial cleavage cleaved unto the odd midnight visitor. This night the odd midnight visitor had left on the outside of almost a quart of port (not to mention the brandy), for such had accompanied his sport.

The lanes were black, unseeable; rain rodded receptive mire underfoot. To cut through Threnody Meadow, in the purlieu of which stood the menhir known as the Stone of Troff, would remove a good mile from Mr. Fox's wearisome plod. His weaving progress, molliwozzled as he was, took him quickly into, and slowly out of, a thicket of thorns, where, the owner oblivious, purse strings were snagged and, as faltering steps carried the fox onward, the purse remained, where it dangled and bobbed merrily from its twig.

The fox saw nothing ahead but blackness, the Stone of Troff forgotten. Stones, it would seem, are fond of reminding forgetful folk of their presence. Short seconds after the purse was lifted, Mr. Fox's sensitive nose renewed its acquaintance with the stone. Lacking in eloquence, the Stone merely conveyed ideas such as "solid" and "immovable," making it a hard lesson to learn.

A root, mischievously hidden beneath a velvety coverlet of moss and impenetrable night, had lain in wait for just such a toe as the fox was then using to stumble blindly forward. The game was afoot, of course.

The concluding prank fell to the stream, swollen with muddy run-off rainwater. It could not resist gurgling the last laugh as it took the rolling tumbler to its bed.

The hall of Westrum Powers was cold as a coffin. The East Anglian skies were leaden, the air was cold and dry. Logs in the great fireplace burned sluggishly, though slightly better than slugs would do in their place. Mr. Pixum was to be found in his study, which was a deal smaller and more easily heated.

'It is only as I expected,' he said to himself, 'the place has been closed up for months. I didn't get out at all last winter, just lounged around blowing bubbles.'

Leaving London for the sticks, he had arranged to meet his friends for moral support at his ancient family seat.

'I'll get some of that mysterious Fenland air into my blood; tackle the problem from a broader perspective.'

Mr. Pixum stared at the map. It was such an effort to concentrate.

'We need to be in a Power Place, somewhere we can cleanse our auras.'

After a frown of indeterminate duration: 'Absorb the great unsullied power of the Sea!'

Mrs. Enderby was in the great kitchen where a roaring fire flourished, unbeknown to Mr. P.

Ovens glowed, pots and pans steamed and bubbled. The kettle sang. The ample woman dabbed her forehead with her pinafore.

'I feel has steamed has a pudd'n. A regiler sticky sausage it is that I ham an' that's the onnist truth.'

Mrs. Enderby's vibrations are, shall we say, solid. Some of us are attuned to the more subtle atmospheres of life, others less so; the housekeeper is, by and (certainly) large, impervious to influences of a tenuous nature although the malaise had not altogether passed by the redoubtable Mrs. E.

Witness the trembling falsetto: 'Oh, I misses 'im so, I do. I misses 'im so. Just comes over me semetimes.'

Mavis Enderby, wife of a permanently missing seaman, blew noisily into her pinny.

'Oh, Billy, are you at rest?' Mrs. E. sniffed.

'Will you hevver come back to me?'

Sniff.

'Hif you walked through this here door right now I'd die stone cold dead, I would.'

Sniff.

'Hif you did that to me I'd give you such a larrupin', let me tell yer! "Don't you dare do that again" I'd say.'

Sniff.

'Oh, what I'd give for the chance to 'ave 'im back 'ome again, my hold man.'

Mr. Pixum's friends had arrived and dined splendidly, courtesy of Mrs. E, therefore, though the doom was upon them, at least they had filled their bellies and discussed their common plight. The Teapot Man, distant cousin (or some such) of Mr. Pixum, spoke of his "un-chocked barrel" interlude after which Mr. Fox told of how he had been set upon and robbed as he returned home from 'a tumbler of sack' at the Chirp.

Their host then told of his bleak condition and they all agreed they were stricken with the same doom and so, unable to fathom it out, they all felt a trifle gleng.

'It may be aimed at us deliberately or it may just be accidental, something we have fallen into, our mutual empathy making it easy for such a thing to catch us altogether,' said Mr. Pixum, 'Surround yourselves with brilliant white light if you can. Close your eyes and imagine it emanating from the crown of your head and enveloping your body like a huge egg, and know that nothing negative can penetrate it.'

He then outlined his plan.

The next morning, provisions packed, they set out for the coast on foot, leaving Mrs E to give Westrum Powers a good scour and polish. By the end of the first day they were exhausted, their spirits lower than ever.

'Lights up ahead,' said Mr. Fox, 'in the trees.'

As they drew closer, they saw the lights actually were up in the trees.

Sitting in the Oaken Tap in Oaken Green, by a fire of apple wood, with good food and drink (the goblets were fashioned to resemble acorn cups), they began to feel better. Thawed out and relaxed, they inspected their surroundings. They were in the most peculiar of inns, nestled as it was in the topmost boughs of an enormous oak that swayed gently at the whim of the wind. Constructed of wood, it had a stone fireplace and chimney. A sign above the mantel read "Never a drop spilled." At a table on the opposite side of the hearth were three locals engaged in a game of Gleek. Occasionally one or other of them could be heard to pronounce 'Tiddy' or 'Tib' or 'Towser' as trumps were called. They were playing for acorns. The innkeeper was a jovial character by the name of Why?tacre. When he wasn't pouring, wiping-up or hauling casks up the tree, he took up his fiddle, sat on a stool and played arboreels.

'Us Why?tacres are descended from tree-faring folk. Reckon that's how I come to have a feel for the fiddle.'

The innkeeper leaned closer to the three travellers (who couldn't help noticing the hundreds of tiny holes dotting his bald head) and spoke in a low voice.

'Tell you something, though. There's something abroad. I can feel it in the tips of my twigs. Can't keep this fiddle in tune for more than forty three minutes at a stretch. And the ale is a demon to keep. Keeps going flat on me, even though I do all I can for it. Aye! Whatever's about, it's detrimental!'

By late afternoon of the second day, the wayfarers reached the coast at Oldbarrow. The light was fading, the tide was out, their spirits were at an even lower ebb.

Oldbarrow is a pleasant town where genteel folk and fisherfolk eke out their days painting watercolours or having watercolours painted of themselves. Our friends stood in the wide High Street eating hot fish pies they had purchased from a pieman with a stall by the Moot Hall. The pavements were lined with an expectant crowd, barely visible in the thickening dusk.

'What is everyone expecting?' asked Mr. Fox of no one in particular.

'Look to your left,' Mr. Pixum nodded, 'Here's your answer.'

A pianoforte sailed gracefully down the middle of the street, followed by a large over-stuffed armchair. Next came a half-tester bed, a wardrobe, a front door, a back door, an attic room, a hall, a bedchamber, a long case clock, a chimney stack, a sash window with curtains and an occasional table. This was too much for Mr. Pixum. He asked a bystander what was going on.

'Oldbarrow Furniture Races o'course,' came the reply, 'Each item powered by invisible mechanisms, driven by a concealed House Jockey. A lot of shellfish changes hands on the outcome of these races. This derby's a big event in these parts.'

The nondescript local had a tendency to be voluble. The gloomy trio drifted away, but not before they heard more about the big event.

'O'course, it's not like it used t'be. It used to be furniture and only furniture, then some Clever Dick changed the rules of entry to "All the House is Eligible." Well, next thing you know they enter the whole house. High Street is known as the Home Straight these days. What's it all coming to? It's not sport any more . . .'

Mr. Pixum led his colleagues northwards, keeping to the beach in the hope that the spiritual essence of the sea would purge the malaise from their souls. A sea mist had crept inland by the time they arrived at the coastal hamlet of Hope Ness forty seven minutes later. There was not the slightest breeze. From here they headed inland, to the west.

Mr. Pixum stopped and motioned to his companions to gather round him. His expression was grave.

This expression left no doubt that he had made a decision, quite an achievement given their current condition.

'I feel we must lose ourselves to The Dark" he said solemnly, "We must lose ourselves in order to find ourselves again.'

'What if all we do is lose ourselves?' asked The Teapot Man.

'There is always a risk,' said Mr. Pixum, 'But after much cogitation I have concluded that we must cease to fight this doom. Give it nothing to push against. It seems to thrive on our resistance. It's like quicksand: the more we struggle, the more we become enmired.'

'Surely,' said Mr. Fox, 'we must try to find out why the world, our world at any rate, has become something less than it was?'

'We shall do that if Fortune favours us. The gathering blackness is pulling us this way. Can you not feel it? Come, we must go to face our doom.'

Mr. Pixum strode into the night.

Deeper and deeper into the dark they walked, through dense woods and reedy fens, though these were sensed more than seen as visibility reached only a few yards. Sounds were dull, there was little to see: a solitary gate, a crumbling flint barn, a dry thorn bush, a stagnant pond. A broken fingerpost to nowhere unbeckoned. Then they were in a thicket of almost impenetrable thorns covered with seaweedlike slime and a dense cold fog. Their spirits were sucked away, leaving them at a new low. The ground beneath their feet was as a sponge that drained their vitality, their consciousnesses became dim, they did not even care. They became apathetic walking dead, their colours drained away, hope drained away. The thought of a hot cup of tea offered to them by a friendly hand, a door opened in welcome, a smile that came from the heart—the stubborn memory of a friendly cup of tea—and all that it meant—brought with it such a rush of emotion that Mr. Fox wept. His heart felt it would break. The Teapot Man wept for the generations of his family who had lived and died in anonymity, always there, behind the scenes, the levers and pivots of the world, unseen and unknown. How had he come to this? He was a failure. Mr. Pixum felt lonely for the first time in his life, as if he were measuring himself with someone else's yardstick. He wept for all the sorrows of the world, for they were all he could think about.

In this silent desert of death, in this dread dark night, in this hopeless world of misery, pain and despair, they presently came upon a dead tree. Grotesque and deformed, it was cloaked in a malevolent fungal growth that glistened and glowed faintly. Through a split in the trunk, between lips of sweating fungus, they saw a cache of musical instruments.

Mr. Pixum, as one in a trance, reached in and pulled out a fiddle and bow. He began with a melancholy air that quickly became a dirge. Mr. Fox took out a horn and joined in. The Teapot Man dragged out a dry old drum and began to beat out a knell. The rhythm quickened. The playing became frenzied. The bow attacked the fiddle, sawing and scraping. From the horn came a staccato series that ended with a mournful wail—and then the sequence was repeated, each time louder than the last. Dust clouds rose from the drum as it thundered and boomed, faster and faster, madder and madder and yet more mad, until utter madness reigned above the blast, the swell, the crescendo. Voices, what voices! An eldritch song formed itself, growing out of the madness, flung from their throats.

'I'll make you thin as I strip your skin
And shave your bones to a powder.
Your weazen I'll rip
To see it drip, drip, drip,
And I always laugh much louder.
I'll dance with glee
As I smash your knee
And drink your brain for an oyster.
Your hide I'll melt,
Wear your ears for a belt
And spew down your gullet as I roister.' [1]

Aeons passed.

Eventually a horrible cadenza drew the cacophony to a close. It ended with a tuneless whine from the fiddle. Mr. Pixum threw the instrument to the ground. His face was grey and his eye possessed a baleful gleam. The fox and The Teapot Man similarly discarded their weapons. "The Song of the Damned"* was over.

The night was hollow but hard, bright with silence, loud without light, soft and fully black. Trees treacly standing, a mass of spongy growth, no green on them. Wraiths moved but could not pass through the trees in silence; they were combed into tatters and coalesced in the clearing.

'We are hollow souls.'

'You are nothing!' Mr. Pixum spat.

'Your soul marches upon your own hollowness.'

'You are dead!' quoth The Teapot Man.

'Not dead—we have only repetition.'

'You are not real!' Mr. Fox barked.

'Life is not real to us.'

'You are nothing and less than nothing!'

'Something, nothing, it's all the same to us.'

Mr. Pixum had descended as far as he could go.

Ascent was now his only choice.

His inner light rested upon a tripod. Nor was it a brass telescope or an oil lamp. It was his essence, upheld by three legs: Persistence, Vision and Courage.

'Look inside yourselves,' he said to his friends, his voice ringing out clear and strong, 'Try to see the malaise—it doesn't show!—you see nothing but boundless aethyr, deep blue empty sky, a realm of infinite possibilities; it is not misery in a box, crammed in tight and reeking! See what you want to see! Feel what you want to feel!'

He smiled a rueful smile.

'It was there all the time; we lost sight of it, that's all. Dreadful mistake! We can perceive the totality of the Multiverse as ranged upon a set of great pianoforte keys at different rates of vibration. Sometimes you get one of your keys jammed and all you can perceive is a sense of unreality, stagnation, sickness—leading to despair, depression, madness. So, in your head, there are all the answers—not merely a soggy walnut marinading inside your cranial pottery. You are more than you can ever think you are. You can be shaken but you *cannot* be broken!'

'He seems quite recovered,' said Mr. Fox, nodding towards Mr. Pixum, 'Although there's an alarming bulge in his cheek.'

'Tongue,' replied The Teapot Man, 'He's certainly found his voice. I think it's time we left this place.'

They had not travelled far when twinkling lights became visible through the trees. A few snowflakes floated airily to the ground. Stars *wheeled* across the face of the heavens.

An exuberance welled up from deep within the three friends, finding expression in a great shout. They were joining in the Green Shout of the Earth, awakened from her winter sleep. The stars joined in and ringing cries echoed eerily about the fens.

Snow began to fall in flurries. With new Light in their hearts they came to a door in a high wall, entered a quiet garden and stepped, with creaking footfalls through the newly fallen snow, towards the welcoming lights of an inn.

Seated before a fire that burned brightly, with as much heat as anyone could possibly ask for, the replete trio called for drinks.

Thelma Teasel, proprietress of the The Lamp of Heaven, wandered over.

'A pot of tea please,' said Mr. Fox.

'Really?' asked Thelma Teasel.

'I jest,' grinned the fox, 'Brandy.'

'Brandy for all!' said Mr. Pixum, 'Will you join us, Thelma Teasel?'

'With pleasure,' she breathed, 'Just as long as you allow me to propose a toast.'

'As you wish,' said Mr. Pixum magnanimously.

'To Light and Life!' declared Thelma Teasel.

'To Light and Life!' agreed her guests.

'More brandy!' demanded fair Thelma Teasel.

---

1. From *'The Dead Pirate Dance'* (Trad. arr. Pixum)

A Fool's Errant

'It would be easier to carry a piglet about, with or without straps,' mused Mr Pixum, 'although a piglet would be most unlikely to serve the same purpose.'

The Vayveltweem Tempyreacon required by, nay, earnestly desired by, Mr Pixum, wasn't a recently created device—others, created with skill and incredible insight by well-intentioned individuals, had appeared from time to time over a number of centuries—but this one had more about it, had more functions, more depth and scope. In short, it was unique. The Namer and the Closer were, in themselves, almost worth having the Vayveltweem for, even if you used it for nothing else.

'But, oh, the elegance of the Vayveltweem Tempyreacon! There really is nothing to touch it,' Mr Pixum said to himself, 'It isn't merely the gleaming planes, the whorls and those clever levers as they move, and make a most satisfying "snick" as they lock, it's the timing of the device! The Vayveltweem creates infinities of possibilities, to be contemplated at leisure, set in motion, realised, all in the space between "tick" and "tock"!'

This longing to possess, this urge to acquire, this desperate need, had grown in the breast of Mr Pixum, scholar, mage, poet and numerous other things that Mr P would no doubt gladly enlarge upon were he asked, from the seed there planted in the form of a message.

The previous day, Monday, Mr Pixum had received a letter from his old friend Alf Middleton. Alf, it transpired, had heard rumours murmured within the arcane circles wherein he moved, that a Vayveltweem Tempyreacon had turned up somewhere in the environs of a small, nondescript town by the name of Eyestone in the county of Leicestershire. By what means it had arrived there, or its exact location, were not known, or if they were, were not mentioned.

A shiver of anticipation had reverberated throughout Mr Pixum's person at this piece of news. He had first read about the Vayveltweem Tempyreacon in a dingy old book he'd picked up in one of the inevitable booksellers in London's Charing Cross Road, entitled *Between Then & Now & Then: The Momentum of the Moment* by Darius D. Ravelle. It had captured his interest entirely. Thoughts of this device had crowded out all other musings and ponderings during each long day ever since. He'd been full of it when last he visited with Alf Middleton, his attentive friend.

'This would be crucial to my research into anything at all!' Mr Pixum enthused, 'This instrument is a kind of "intent-measuring gauge" and lots more besides—with the means to calibrate and evaluate the amount of originality and individuality contained in a particular intent!'

Mr Pixum strode back and forth, conducting his passion with dramatic waving of arms, his hands slicing the supramundane woodsmoke of Alf Middleton's penumbral parlour.

'You must see the usefulness of the thing? You can determine the wisdom of carrying the intent through, do you see? Has the intent reached sufficient intensity to enable it to "actuate"? And there's more to it than that! I simply must lay my hands on this device!'

Mr Middleton, after the conversation had eventually descended to more easily digested topics, namely rabbit pie epulated with a jug of dark ale, and leave-taking was imminent, had promised to keep his ear to the ground in the unlikely event that mention of the whereabouts of this almost-fabled Vayveltweem Tempyreacon should occur. Well, now it had occurred and there was only one thing to do. Mr Pixum packed his carpet bag and set off in horse-unravelling haste.

Scything the leagues westwards through the Shires, it still took him three days to cover the distance. Mr Pixum arrived, aching and tired, in Eyestone early on a Thursday evening. In the failing light his impression was of an unremarkable town, neither large nor small, possessing no discernible charm while at the same time it was not eye-warpingly hideous, merely vulgar. It seemed to Mr P that it existed in a kind of limbo, a town on the edge of everything and nothing.

While strolling the darkening streets, he sensed that instead of pleasant anticipation for the evening to come, whether of a well-earned rest from the day's labours or a night's lovemaking or junketing, the inhabitants emanated a distinct lack of vibrancy, of *joie de vivre*, as Mr Fox would say. Mr Pixum saw men and women, young and old, lurking indolently on street corners and in doorways, peering shamelessly at each other, their eyes darting like busy ants hither and yon, making no secret of their interest in the turpitude of their fellows, consumed by an insatiable desire to know everyone else's business, indifferent to being about their own. It was as if the people in this part of the world had forgotten how to enjoy the finer things offered by being alive and had chosen to claw out an existence that had, as its pinnacle, the mere satisfaction of primitive needs—and this an end in itself.

This was disconcerting.

Bats fluttered mousily in and out of the gothic tracery fringing the cupola of an odd-looking bandstand in the market square. Dogs slunk around corners, furtive shadows within shadows; he overheard a couple of lurchers discoursing upon how, in his cups at the races, one of them had paid for a tip from a "coat tugger," how it turned out this rogue had been "in" with the Clerk of the Scales and something about the yearling being "scratched" at the last minute. They disappeared into a tavern, leaving their cigar smoke writhing in the doorway like a stale phantom.

'The market place is not exactly teeming with folk,' thought Mr Pixum, 'and everyone abroad appears so resolute, so impatient. I fear they won't have the time to listen to me, much less spare the time to help me find what I'm looking for.'

He stood amongst the stalls and gazed about. A stream trickled by only a short distance from the Market Square. Lanterns twinkled above the wares and traders cajoled, busked, flattered and threatened the few indifferent townsfolk who passed by. He wandered on and presently found himself in the High Street. He spotted the lights of an inn about a hundred yards away and headed for it.

'Maybe I'll find some obliging company in there,' he thought.

Sitting snugly by the fireside in the frowzy, musty smelling back room of the Bull and Mouth Inn, Mr Pixum summoned enough effort to succeed in putting his recent experience behind him.

'I should have guessed that would happen,' he thought, 'I was so wrapped up in my enthusiasm I didn't give it a thought. Such derision though! I never was so mocked. The very mention of a Vayveltweem Tempyreacon, which, in me, induces shivers of excitement, in these down-to-earth folk produces howls of ridicule! Life can be such a crook-backed carrot at times.'

Taking a sip of his port he stared into the flames and pondered.

Almost as soon as he'd entered the Tap Room an oaf had declared that Mr Pixum 'had the nose of a perfect English stranger!' and another had pronounced him as 'about as bright as new pig' and then went on to tell him to mind his own business, 'You walk in here as large as lice, poking your carrot in where it's not welcome. I don't know who you are, but let me tell you this: Look before you leek from now on,' tapping his nose, 'Let that be a worm in your ear.'

'Well, that was,' thought Mr Pixum, 'not quite the worm I was hoping for, whether in urea or not.'

He had asked the landlord if there was somewhere more private (and out of range of further impertinence); thankfully he was directed into this relatively comfortable parlour.

Warmed by the fire and calmed by the silence, which was of a very dead kind, into which the tickings and tockings of the clock plummeted, Mr Pixum began to feel his composure return. His mind was once again free to rove. His thoughts turned inevitably to the Vayveltweem Tempyreacon. What, exactly, would he do with such a thing?

'I can imagine it being useful for so many things,' he thought, 'such as . . .'

Several minutes skipped, hobbled and crept by as the mage, the scholar, the protean Feather of Fate attempted to conjure up things he could do with the Vayveltweem Tempyreacon, an exercise that required more effort than he expected.

'I could ask D'Arcy Gammon, the odd jobber, to, shall we say, collect some books I very urgently require for my studies, then I could turn on the Vayveltweem Tempyreacon and he'd return ten minutes before he left. Ten minutes is a guess. Perhaps I'd berate him for his tardiness, without realising that it could only bring Gammon back four minutes before he set off. Poor Gammon! He would find himself placing my parcel of books on my desk with no idea of how he came to be doing it, and then, ten or four or however many minutes afterwards, he would, at my instruction, be setting off to fetch them!'

Mr Pixum smiled at the thought of this time-saving peculiarity.

'D'Arcy Gammon, being a punctual man, would be somewhat confused by this. I can anticipate his dismay: "It puts the tone of my day all at sixes and seven-eighths," he would say and I would attempt to resolve his discomfort by handing him the wherewith-all to take himself off to the Clockmaker's Hands, there to sample the earthy delights dispensed therein.'

A sigh. 'Heigh ho.'

'But what else could I use it for?'

Mr P ploughed on with his train of thought, his brow furrowed.

'I recall that Ravelle, in his book, writes that it "verifies . . . and something or other . . . the individuality and individual freedom of Sentientkind as a whole"—or was it something else?

'How I wish The Teapot Man were here! I could discuss it all with him and we'd have the thing to rights in no time at all! Ah, time. Now that is something The Teapot Man knows about in his own peculiar way. If he were here now he'd tell me how his mind can grasp each minute facet of each minute at the same time as it grasps the whole multitudinous percept of the, er, whole—the "worm's eye view" and the "bird's eye view" simultaneously. He *understands* and *overstands*! Yet it would not be inaccurate to aver that The Teapot Man's diligent labours are nothing more than revisions, double-checking broad and also razor-narrow concepts which, Heaven help us, he already knows! His studies of Time alone are cyclopean—he spent months studying seconds, minutes, hours, days and weeks—then he spent years studying months! As he says "Rome wasn't built in a daze."

'"Sometimes it takes time to time time but it is extremely rewarding from time to time,"' whatever The Teapot Man means by *that*. I know we seem to have quick time and slow time. "Time flies when you're ecstatic, though not always," et cetera. We have the dubious objective time and the familiar subjective time. We can do something about this subjective time. This is down to our perception. We can transform minutes into hours if we become enraptured by a rose or bemused by a bumble bee—and sometimes the opposite is true—what seemed but a minute was an hour that flew away, transformed by exaltation. Quite. Look also at time itself as a transformer: The immediacy of incidents often hides their importance. A decent period of elapsed time helps to place these happenings into their historical context. We can step back and see how various events relate to each other. Patterns emerge. Layers of interpretation slide over the facts. This is what history, as known and told by most sentient beings at any rate, *is*. The hard, cold facts, in the present in which they happen are likely to seem depressing, irritating, sordid, cruel, insignificant even, but whatever they *do* seem, they will rarely glow and fizz with that magical golden light in which legend and myth are bathed, a gift bestowed upon events in time by time itself.'

Mr Pixum yawned.

'I am getting nowhere, thinking away like this, all alone. I need Bertie Fox here to throw in an irreverent remark now and then, just to keep my feet on the floor.'

Mr Pixum came slowly back to full wakefulness with a strange dream of huge red wings flapping over him.

A voice cried out: 'A bottle of your best wine, landlord! And something on a plate to wash down with it!'

He opened his eyes to full darkness.

'By the soaring music inherent in Greek sunlight!' exclaimed Mr Pixum, 'Is that you, Bertie?'

'Eh? *Pardon*? Who the Dickens . . ?'

Mr Fox's penny dropped and with a flourish he removed his coat from Mr Pixum's head.

'There you are Pixum! Sorry about that! Thought you'd've gone off and found yourself a bed by now!'

'What are you doing here?' asked Mr Pixum, not trying to contain his surprise and finding the wash of cold air tumbling from his friend's apparel not entirely welcome.

'Bumped into Mr Middleton a couple of days ago, heard what was afoot, jumped aboard the Mail and *voila*! *Je suis ici*! Any luck finding this Go-between whatsit?'

Was Mr Fox's open countenance nothing more than a mask of irony, Mr Pixum wondered, or was it simply what it appeared to be on the face it? Was that glint in his eyes nothing more than high spirits? It was like attempting to lip-read a flea. Knowing this rascal as well as he did, Mr P decided to err on the cynical side.

'What do you think?' he asked.

'Come outside for a tick and then tell me what *you* think,' replied Mr Fox with a barely discernible leer, 'Come on! Don't dawdle!'

This last as Mr Pixum struggled with his coat.

Emerging from the inn, Mr Pixum saw a sky speckled with stars, saw thatched roofs limned with starlight, saw owls, chimney pots, dolphins, teapots, a herm of Typhon, triumphal arches, watchhouses, observatories, doric entabulature, a statue of Kneph Mendes, all crazed silverly by the light of a Teapot Moon, and saw . . . The Teapot Man!

Standing across the street, barely visible in the obscurity of nightshadows, the diminutive figure with more stars gleaming in the red teapot upon his head than there are wasps around a syllabub, beckoned Mr Pixum to him.

'Double *voila!*' said The Teapot Man, mysteriously referring to Mr Fox's previous *frenchism*, as he stepped aside, revealing a shop window.

An old curiosity shop, noted Mr Pixum, without a trace of irony. His eye accustomed to the dark, he saw a strange object within, taking pride of shadowy place among various pieces of bric á brac.

The gleaming planes! The whorls! The levers!

Sitting there "as large as lice" was the Vayveltweem Tempyreacon. It had, Mr Pixum noticed, a tired label tied to it, off-handedly bearing the scrawl "*Harness adornment? Samovar? Horologe? £5 —*"

Mr Pixum's heart pounded like a galloping elephant's foot umbrella stand, his palms clammy. At last the object of his desire was there before him. Staring at it, expression slowly drained from his countenance.

Wondering what could have inspired anyone to guess that strange-looking device might possibly be a "harness adornment," The Teapot Man took Mr Pixum gently by the elbow and guided him through the doorway, into the flickering lamplight of the shop's interior. The proprietor stood in his nightshirt, half hidden by haphazard clutter, holding the lamp; his discomfiture at being wrenched from his bed was plain to see.

Mr Pixum reached out a hand and touched the device gingerly. With a fingertip he traced the Namer and the Closer. He touched a lever. It snicked. He felt nothing.

Mr Pixum had a vision.

A brittle structure fashioned from antimony, which was quite obviously a rendering of a rending antinomy, appeared brazenly to his inward gaze. The desire to cut corners. The desire to be true. Tension vibrated throughout the glittering latticework. It thrummed with the uncontainable dichotomy. With a wracking shudder the dam betwixt the two opposites burst. The structure was swept away.

A great wave of anticlimax swallowed him up.

In Elysium, an asphodel bloomed.

Mr Fox and The Teapot Man flanked their friend before the fire in the snug of the Bull and Mouth Inn. Both looked at Mr Pixum. The Teapot Man's expression contained elements of compassion, humour, severity and the usual madness, topped-off with a wry smile. The fox showed insouciance, amusement, impatience, the desire to have done with it. Was there a soupçon of sympathy in *les yeux jaunes du renard*?

'The truth is,' said Mr Pixum, quivering, feeling shame, absolutely *not himself*, 'I have no use for the thing. I sat in the snug, alone, thinking and thinking and, I don't know what happened; I must have dozed off, and now, as I recall the thoughts I had, helped out by you, Teepeeyem . . .'

'I know,' put in The Teapot Man, softly patting Mr P's shoulder.

'. . . and you, Bertie, helping with my rude awakening, I realised I had no need of any such contraption—I can do more or less everything it purports to do all by myself! It seemed so . . . *amazing* when I read about it. Now it seems nothing more than an irrelevance. Originality, individuality, intentionality: all are born within. This device is to semiempiricism what hubris is to a false avatar. Who really needs to have books delivered before they are sent for? Though it did bring us together around this jolly fire . . . perhaps it was of some use after all.'

The device, nevertheless, sat on their table amid bottles, glasses and plates, performing the office of hatstand for Bertie Fox's cocked hat; his wits somewhat pendular, Mr Pixum had felt obliged to purchase the thing after his friends had put the shopkeeper to such inconvenience . . .

'That thing's about as much use as a minute hand on a second-hand teapot!' said Mr Fox, firing up his pipe and tossing a still-smoking spill on to the hearth, 'We have no need of an excuse to get together, *mon ami.*'

'You wouldn't have used the device very often anyhow,' said The Teapot Man, 'It is very heavy on *ground abscontius*. And a flask of Lassiter's "Temps Perdew" costs the earth and lasts for no time at all.'

'Never mind flasks of ground abscontius!' barked Mr Fox, 'Landlord! Bring forth another steaming bowl of your excellent punch this very minute!'

❧ ✣ ☙

Mr Pixum came slowly back to full wakefulness with a strange dream of huge red wings flapping over him.

A voice cried out: 'A bottle of your best wine, landlord! And something on a plate to wash down with it!'

He opened his eyes to full darkness.

'By the soaring music inherent in Greek sunlight!' exclaimed Mr Pixum, 'Is that you, Bertie?'

Note: Tempyreacons are known to have existed in Chaldea in the 3rd Century BCE when Ozmian Tempionics were at their zenith. Humbert "Cloud Chaser" Vayveltweem, elaborating upon the original concept, developed this particular device in the mid-16th Century EV after failing to perfect "circumspective mercury."

One Last Summer at World's End

No one expected the Dead Pyrate to up and leave the Curiosity Shop where he'd been gathering dust for years, but that is exactly what he did.

Leaving the door to creak to behind him, he stumped off along the street, past shops and inns which, under the assault of neglect and weather, resembled nothing so much as a row of crumbling sea biscuits. Clump, thock! Clump, thock! he went. Clump! Thock!

Mr Pixum, mage, mystic, scholar, was picking pixie caps. Mr Pixum knew why they were known as "pixie caps": he had worn such a cap as a child, being of the pixie race. The fungi were for his niece, Lucinda, who used them to augment her shamanic practices. Out of nowhere came a moment when he saw something unaccountable. For no apparent reason he looked up at the sky and there it was—or seemed to be. No doubt it must mean something.

'True, but doesn't everything? Alright, it must be something ominous, maybe something that is already occurring.'

The sun was shining and in all other respects the day appeared innocent enough.

'Of course,' he thought, admiring a stand of beeches on the hilltop, 'this is just me being gloomy. I hope I'm wrong. Whatever it is, I may as well collect a few more of these pesky, evasive pixie caps and enjoy what remains of the afternoon.'

It had been a long summer, sometimes sunshine, sometimes wet, but the pasture in which he gathered the dainty ivory buttons was always quite damp due to the spring that seeped above the field's slope and irrigated it gently; occasionally Lucinda's horses, Bonny and Todd, were brought here for the grazing. This year's crop of mushrooms was early and already abundant; even so they took some hunting down. Lucinda, who was undertaking a systematic study of certain oblique dimensions, would appreciate a fresh supply of pixie caps. These she used to facilitate entry into some of the more elusive realms. There was ample time to dry them out before her return.

Rubbing the small of his back, he straightened and looked around the meadow. A scattering of flowers still bloomed, campion, scabious, centaury, mallow, like spots of paint on a green canvas; hardly a hint of autumn gold in the hedgerow; the only sounds were waves rumbling gently at the foot of the cliffs, the murmur of lazy insects and the occasional cry of a gull. From his viewpoint he could see only the divisions between grassy cliff top, tranquil sea and the sky, pale blue on the horizon and deepening towards cobalt at its zenith. The immediate air was redolent of sun-warmed grasses allowing but a hint of the salty sea to impinge.

'No other time of year can match the light and grace of an Indian Summer,' thought Mr Pixum as he stooped for his trug.

'A brigantine, she looks like,' said The Teapot Man aloud. He stood on Trefusis Point above the hamlet of Flushing, gazing into a sky that arched over the great shipping inlet of Carrick Roads. Looking into this wide emptiness was not strictly a part of The Teapot Man's current self-imposed study, which was to scrutinise the rooftops of Falmouth from this vantage point at different times of the day and to extract the aesthetic meaning therefrom. The scrutinising of airborne sea-vessels was a permissible exception.

The floating ship was above and beyond Falmouth town. She was so high in fact, that she was no more than a fleck in the wide blue Cornish sky.

The Teapot Man, The *legendary* Teapot Man, wore an upturned teapot upon his head, this exotic millinery was in the style of the Oriental Yixing crossed with the globular English vernacular, made from a unique clay and glazed in a bright red. It was rumoured to be indicative of his essential purpose. Gossips had hinted at the possibility of Oriental connections. Of his green greatcoat and red trousers, nothing was said.

Displaying his remarkable agility, Mr Fox wove his way through the crowd hurling and burling about Market Strand. He moved with speed and fluidity, his bushy tail a well-groomed wake. He stood out a bright jewel among the generally more restrained shades of the throng about him, his red hunting coat worn unbuttoned and waistcoat of bright mustard hue lending him the air of a dandy, which was, after all, his intent.

It was some time since Mr Fox had sported a hat but lately the desire to be seen beneath one had grown more insistent. It was sheer vanity, he knew, but when had he ever let that concern him? Somewhere in the jostling streets of Falmouth was a hatter's shop. This was something he believed rather than knew, being a fox who expected Life to provide for his needs punctually. Although this was not always the case, Life came through for him more often than not. The nuances of this were not lost upon him; he knew he owed many of his pranks and exhibitions of suavity to this belief. It was this ingrained knack that enabled him to fling his cane across a room the instant a servant would walk through the door and catch it; throw his coat on to a peg without a glance; passing the fireplace, he would snatch the spill from the hapless fellow who had just lit it, light his pipe and hand it back in time to whip a glass from the proffered drinks tray and launch into an amusing anecdote—all without a pause. This kind of entrance, although he would never show it, left him licitly pleased with himself.

Passing a bookseller's, he was struck by a sudden fancy to read a salty, seafaring tale that would add a little more depth to his relish of the Cornish ambience. He slipped inside.

The aroma of old bindings almost induced a sneeze. Here they were! *Mr Midshipman Easy! Robinson Crusoe! Moonfleet! Treasure Island!* Mr Fox eagerly reached for the latter. What was this? At his touch the volume powdered into snuff.

⌘ ✝ ⌘

Having threaded his harvest of pixie caps on to lengths of cotton and hung them to dry from beams in Lucinda's kitchen, Mr Pixum walked out into the cottage garden and lit his pipe. Less unaccountable now because her sail was visible, the mysterious ship was approaching from the east. Although the air had acquired a chill from the incipient evening, he stayed in the garden, looking up into the sky, thinking while he smoked.

Edges bright in the westering sun, strange layers of cloud resembling tide-rippled sand had surged across the blue. Sailing above the clouds, the ship was clearly visible through the striations of vapour. She had increased in size. There was no doubt now: she was a full-rigged brigantine, silvery as a pale moon. Gracefully she descended through a layer of cirro-cumulus and sailed on.

Mr Pixum continued to stare.

Almost imperceptibly she dropped through several more unusual layers of cirrus, parting the wispy strands as if cruising through a tropical sea, until she was free of all cloud.

Mr Pixum could make out her stern lanterns as they glowed in the deepening dusk.

A man sat in a darkened room. He was very still. The shutters were closed even though it was only late afternoon and nightfall was yet hours away. The shutters had been closed all day. They had been closed for several days. His loaf sat on the table untouched, stale. His jaw was clamped tight, giving his under-bite undue emphasis. His ears, large and rounded, were being used to hold back lank hair from his face. He could hear the comings and goings down below.

The floorboards were thin, and in one or two places where the boards had shrunk, he could see vague movement through the gaps if he looked carefully. He heard an exclamation from someone in the room beneath him. Not understanding the words, he could, nevertheless, hear them clearly.

'*Il s'est transformé en poussiere!*'

As The Teapot Man returned across the river towards Falmouth, he once again glanced at the sky. The brigantine was now much closer. The ferryman, following The Teapot Man's gaze, nodded and spat a plug of tobacco into the river.

'What d'ye reckon o' yon percoolier clowd? Do 'im be a omen or summat?'

Without replying, The Teapot Man merely met the ferryman's eye.

'Bah!" said the ferryman with a snort of contempt, 'T'en't n'more'n a blasted ol' clowd not worth a fuss!'

A high keening caught The Teapot Man's pointy ear, drawing his attention out in the direction of the Carrick Roads.

Hanging in the air above the waters was a host of tall, gaunt figures with great gauzy wings. Around them an unearthly light glowed. They blew trumpets of gold, producing the eerie fanfare.

The Teapot man shivered.

''Tis a dread vision,' said he.

With bulging eyes, the ferryman pulled frantically at the oars.

'"*Ha! Ha! quoth he, full plain I see,*
The Devil knows how to row!"' [4]

quoted The Teapot Man, grinning to himself.

'Heralds?' he thought, 'Or something else?'

Mr Fox turned to find the bookseller and his assistant staring at him.

He felt needlessly guilty and decidedly foolish.

'I merely attempted to retrieve the book.'

He forced his countenance into a stern expression.

'Do you have an infestation of Worm?'

Bookworm could, after all, spell the end for a bookseller.

The bookseller, a sturdy young man, shook black unruly curls from his forehead and started towards the fox.

'What have you done?' His dark eyes burned.

'I merely touched the book,' replied Mr Fox.

'My books are in fine condition!' the bookseller said, his brows meeting angrily, 'There's no Worm on these premises!'

The fox, having regained his composure, flicked at the pile of dust that had so recently been *Treasure Island*.

'Then how do you explain this? Come and look for yourself.'

The bookseller stood by the shelf, looking from Mr Fox to the powdered book with a suspicious eye. His assistant had stepped close behind him. Mr Fox could not help noticing how attractive she was, her chestnut hair cascaded over her shoulders and her scent was sensual and enticing. She reminded him of a vixen he once knew.

'You'll have to pay for the damage,' stated the bookseller.

'*Moi?*' exclaimed Mr Fox, 'You don't seriously believe . . .'

'Stay, Oliver!' cut in the girl assistant, 'Will you look at its neighbours? Do they remain intact?'

Oliver, the bookseller, reluctantly removed his glare from the fox and attempted to remove *Robinson Crusoe*.

'It's crumpled!' he gasped.

A Tale of Pyrates was next to fall in a heap, swiftly followed by Swift's *Gulliver's Travels*, Byron's *The Corsair*, *Moonfleet* by J Meade Falkner, Sterne's *The Life and Opinions of Tristram Shandy, Gentleman* and, inexplicably, J B Craven's *Doctor Robert Fludd*.

'It can't be!' shouted the bookseller.

In frustration he swept a large hand along the shelf to left and right. Clouds of choking dust filled the air.

Mr Pixum sprawled in his chair and stared into the fire, puzzling himself into tangles about the appearance in the sky. The pheasant that Lucinda's housekeeper was roasting for supper permeated the parlour with a most pleasant aroma. The others would be home soon enough—and hungry to boot.

As was his habit, he wore his tweed coat and top hat indoors, his pointed ears splaying out beneath the brim. With his eye-patch and gaunt frame his distinctive figure not only made sprawling look respectable but also fashionable.

'Ah, well,' he murmured at length, 'we've had a jolly good summer down here in Cornwall.'

His niece had invited her uncle 'Poddy' and his friends to stay at her cottage near the village of Mawnan Smith while she was away studying on the Continent.

'Lucinda will appreciate the pixie caps,' he thought, 'She'll be home soon. I'll miss it down here, but . . .' Looking at his barely detectable paunch, he sighed, 'I won't miss the food.' He smiled. 'There's too much of it and it's too good to pass over!'

The three stood outside the shop, their backs to the window in order to avoid being jostled on the crowded street. Seafarers, merchants, urchins, ladies with servants, milled on the cobbles, dodging the carriages and carts that clattered and clopped between them. In the air hung the humid aroma of horse dung.

Full introductions had now been made. Oliver Probus and Aliya Haddaway, his assistant, were lovers and were shortly to wed.

'What shall I do?' the bookseller asked Mr Fox.

'I know what I should do,' replied Mr Fox, patting dust from his sleeves with a pair of white gloves, 'I should lock up the shop, move to a quiet village and keep chickens.' A speculative glint flickered fleetingly in the fox's eyes.

Oliver Probus looked about to lose the temper he had so recently almost found.

'Alright!' said Mr Fox placatingly, 'There must be a cure for it. I don't know what it might be but I'll try to help you. I have some very good friends. We can put our heads together and perhaps get to the bottom of it. Meanwhile I suggest you go back inside and sweep up the dust.'

He took a bow.

'Now I must be away!'

'Where are you going?' asked Aliya Haddaway, fearfulness darkening her green eyes.

'To the hatter's. *Au revoir!*'

The mystical Mr Pixum had descended into a deep, fire-warmed stupor. He was enjoying this lassitude unashamedly when he was instantly snapped out of it by:

> *"Fifteen men on The Dead Man's Chest—*
> *Yo-ho-ho, and a bottle of rum!"*

Through the still evening, a rousing chorus echoed above Mawnan Smith, above the blackbird's evening benediction, above the lowing of cattle, above the housemaid's shriek.

> *"Drink and the devil had done for the rest—*
> *Yo-ho-ho, and a bottle of rum!"*

Awe stamped upon his lean features, Mr Pixum stood in the garden, looking upwards. A hundred and fifty yards above, sailing majestically through the sunset sky, was not only the brigantine, *Queen Anne's Revenge*, the flagship of Edward Teach, otherwise known as Blackbeard, but the *Hispaniola* and a huge number of other sail, all flying a version of the Jolly Roger. And there, in this great ghostly flotilla was *The Golden Hind*, the ship of El Draque, along with the ships of Captain Henry Morgan, Bartholomew Roberts, Anne Bonney, the Killigrews, Mary Read, Grany Malley and all the pyrates, privateers, buccaneers, cut-throats and rogues ever to rollick upon the High Seas. Even that curséd ship and its Mariner, whose albatross "*about his neck was hung.*"

Mr Pixum was shocked to the core of his being when, with evil emphasis, a pyrate aboard the Hispaniola, it could only have been Israel Hands, hailed him thus:

'Ahoy Pixum! C'm'ere me beauty an' I'll give ye a taste o' the Cap'n's Daughter!'

Beside him, an amused Long John squinted knowingly.

'"*Fifteen men on The Dead Man's Chest—*
Yo-ho-ho, and a bottle of rum!"'

The ditty was taken up by all hands as more and more vessels descended through the cloud-seas of light and mist.

'"*Drink and the devil had done for the rest—*"'[1]

Now bilander, now brigantine, now galliot, shallop and hoy; the luminous evening resonated with voices roistering in rich, deep unison.

The Teapot Man had come ashore and wandered the streets for a while before taking refreshment in the Queen's Arms, which seemed somehow 'grainy' and flat. He put that observation aside for now while he considered the meaning of his recent vision.

'I believe it may be The Last Trump,' he concluded, 'and if so, is it somehow connected to my more recent discovery?'

En route to his watering hole, he had been strolling along a decrepit street when he happened upon a Curiosity Shop. He stepped inside and as his eyes became accustomed to the gloom he saw that which only his trained eyes could see: a Dead-Pyrate-shaped hole surrounded by bric à brac, curios and junk.

'We didn't expect him to just up and leave,' said the proprietor, a threadbare orang-utan wearing an orange pea-coat, 'He's been here gathering dust for years.'

Before the mirror stood Mr Fox. He pulled the hat forward, set it square between his ears, tipped it jaunty to one side, then the other, pushed it back, pulled it forward again. It was elegant, gentlemanly, dashing, the new look, black, shiny, brimmed. All these things the Hatter had assured him. The mirror, though, did not or could not lie.

The fox hissed through his teeth.

'*Non!*'

'I beg your pardon, sir?' The Hatter hovered.

Under his breath, Mr Fox growled, '*Je me sens idiot dans un chapeau haut de forme!*' and skimmed the hat towards its purveyor who reached out to catch it before it did any damage to itself or to himself.

The Hatter winced as the door slammed.

He continued to sit in the dark. He could taste the acrid dust that had floated up through the floorboards. He neither knew nor cared what had taken place below. Only one thing had quickened his pulse, and deepened, if it were possible, his pain. The sound of her voice, so close to him and now so far away.

With an exasperated 'Huff!' Mr Fox preened his lapels and cuffs, smoothed his whiskers and strode along the street. It was now twilight, the street was in shadow, the lamps not yet lit.

A sharp pain exploded in his head. This was followed by a ringing sound. Something glinted by his foot. Holding his head, the fox scrabbled about the cobbles for the shiny object. It was a heavy, golden earring.

'Certainly packed a wallop. Where did that come from?'

He looked up. And saw the eerie flotilla sailing low above the town.

'*Par la théière sacrée!*' he exclaimed. Turning on his heel, he re-entered the Hatter's.

Ten minutes later, Mr Fox made a flit down by the King's Pipe, the better to espy the uncanny seadogs. What to make of all this? *Alors!* He must relate this to Pixum. Floating above the harbour, the ships were dropping anchor through air briny and cool. Already a higgledy-piggledy mass of masts and rigging, this was chaos. Wavelets of breeze lapped hulls encrusted with barnacles, pyrate crews cat-called and spat with gusto, jolly boats lowered by ropes slapped into the water, oars pulled them to shore. The sound of roistering was everywhere. He didn't hear the Clump, thock! Clump, thock! until too late.

When he came to, his head was spinning. He could hear Clump, thock! Clump, thock! dying into the distance.

Picking up his battered new hat, he fled.

The Teapot Man turned a corner and almost lost his head.

Cutlass flashing, fuses sparking and fizzing in his beard and hair, here was Edward Teach, the infamous Blackbeard, as ever he was. Looking frisky as a walrus with a hedgehog in his breeches, the reek of rum and gunpowder wafted about him.

'Scurvy pothead!' roared Blackbeard, eyes mad and burning, 'I'll sharpen yer neck and use yer for a quill-pen! Ah ha!'

The Teapot Man, in a rare moment of decisiveness, ran away.

'So . . . let me get this straight,' said Mr Pixum, 'Falmouth is now a pyrate's junket, books have disintegrated in Oliver Probus's bookshop and The Teapot Man has had a vision of The Last Trump. Is that how the land lies?'

The three friends were reunited in the parlour of Lucinda's cottage. Roast pheasant had been appreciated and the fire was hearty. Mr Fox and The Teapot Man were sitting either side of the fire and Mr Pixum was stalking back and forth between them.

Mr Fox shrugged.

'Not quite. Some of Probus's books have powdered, that is true; the pyrates are marauding in the town, that is also true, but there is the other thing I noticed which is worse, I think.' He began stuffing his pipe.

'Let's have it, then!' Mr Pixum demanded, standing over the fox.

'It's as if the world is . . .' he searched for the words, 'It is the fading of things. Less substantial. Everywhere. More around the bookseller's though.' The fox rose to his feet, snatched up a spill and lit his pipe from the fire. Aromatic smoke hung in hammocks of air in a manner that could only be described as "comfortable".

The Teapot Man added: 'I too, noticed things were lacklustre, sort of grainy.' He sat up and uncrossed his legs, in his teapot's glaze reflected firelight danced. 'I felt for the Threads of Fate, there was nothing; I thought to consult the tea-leaves only to find sludge in my cup.'

Mr Pixum smoked his pipe and stared out of the window into darkness. The only sounds were the occasional settling of a log on the fire, the creaking of furniture and the ticking of the mantel clock. At length, Mr Pixum ceased his pacing, pulled up a chair and sat down.

Bleakly he announced, 'I am certain we have an Eater of Worlds on our hands.'

He drained his port before directing a piercing glance at each of his colleagues.

'There is no time to lose! If I am correct in my deduction, everything is at stake—I mean *everything*!'

He rose to his feet. 'The Last Trump has heralded the End of Things.' He tapped out his pipe against the fireplace. 'First, though, there is something I must explain to you. The quickest way to do this, I believe, is to give you a little demonstration.'

He disappeared into the kitchen, returned swiftly and dropped a heap of pixie caps on the tabletop. Deftly, he separated them into three equal portions.

'Eat!' said Mr Pixum. 'Look lively! Our very existence is threatened!'

Mystified, his two friends joined him at the table and reluctantly began munching the tiny fungi.

'Bit gritty,' mumbled the Teapot Man.

Mr Pixum fetched a flagon of cider from the larder.

'Wash 'em down with this.'

As the last pale mushroom slipped into Mr Fox's throat, Mr Pixum began to speak.

'There are many and various worlds, or *univi* as I prefer to call them, that exist within the Omni, the multiverse.'

'The planets?' asked Mr Fox.

'Maybe,' replied Mr Pixum mysteriously, 'but not necessarily.'

They resumed their seats by the fire.

'There are univi as you know, where worlds of every conceivable kind abide. The pixie caps will assist my demonstration and will serve us well in the next few hours.'

Mr Pixum stood.

'We now await their effect and have time to make ready Lucinda's gig. Bertie, I'll help you bring it round. Teapot Man, fetch Bonny from the pasture and harness her up. Take a handful of feed; as you know, she's sometimes difficult to catch.' He made for the door, saying, 'Now I have a couple of things to fetch from my trunk'.

When Bonny was put to the gig, Mr Pixum observed his friends who by now were somewhat beatific and vague.

'Don't fasten the girth too tight too quickly!,' he said, 'And for Odin's sake check the breaching's going to be safe on the hills. We have a journey of two leagues and an appointment with Fate.'

Presently, the trio returned to the parlour, complete with dilated stares and beaming grins—the pixie caps had taken hold.

'To continue,' began Mr Pixum, his features struggling to maintain a serious expression, 'We have, for example, the World of Highwaymen, the World of Gypsies, the World of Pyrates and . . .' Mr Pixum turned down the lamp and snuffed the candles, 'the

World of Robin Hood. Behold!'

He gestured towards the corner of the room where the grandfather clock stood invisible in the shadows.

> *"'At eventide rides Robin Hood homeward from his quest;"*
> recited Mr Pixum,
> *"'A wayward breeze bestirs his locks; he winds his bugle-horn.*
> *He bids his Merry Men return, for the sun sinks in the west:*
> *From byway and brake they come, through oak and birch and thorn.'"*

From the darkness in the corner grew a light, at first nothing but a speck growing, glowing with colours bright as jewels, forming a mandala-like pattern, then spinning, brighter and brighter, larger and larger until it became as a window through which they could see sunlight among leaves; cow-parsley, woodbine and wild rose in their Midsummer glory, their flowers perfuming the fresh woodland air. Something, (a light breeze?) stirs the hawthorn bushes which stand beneath towering oaks.

> *"'The outlaws' day is done, Robin and his merry thieves*
> *Gather in their shadowed haunt, full hearty in their strumméd lays,*
> *Made mythic by the magick among the wildwood leaves.*
> *Scarlock, Tuck, Little John and all, sing 'round the cheery blaze.'"*

A movement, as if part of the greenwood has taken flight; the figure is just discernible, clad in the colours of the forest, the motion lithe and graceful as a deer, smooth as a squirrel, quick as a wren. Then all is still. Suddenly, a green-clad outlaw raises up his horn and winds a long resounding note that reverberates out into the forest, echoing until it slowly dies away. The scene changes to a glade where the onlookers see a host of merry fellows standing, lying, chatting quietly. From a cooking fire, tendrils of wood-smoke rise into the leaves high above. Here and there lookouts can be discerned among oak boughs soaring overhead. The band turn as one to greet a man who has appeared silently in their midst. He takes in his comrades with a sweep of his arm and laughs. The laughter echoes about the glade and is taken up by all present. Around the fire a lute is played, the men sing along lustily. From somewhere above, a silvery chorus is heard but faintly.

"'Marian sings of branches entwined against the sky,
Among the leaves so dense perch Fair Folk ever sly,
With radiant wings of gauze, red caps and moonstone eyes,
Their bandy legs a-swing, tiny throats a-trill, their faces grin awry."' [2]

The scene fades away and the room is left in darkness. Until . . .

"'O goat-foot God came I to see
At dusky eve and dewy dawn!
Upon the slopes of Arkady
Dance maenad, satyr, nymph and faun;"'

Light once again appears in the corner of the room, flaring up into a scene of a hillside. Bright sunlight creates dappled shadows beneath olive trees and the resinous scent of cypress is carried on waves of heat through the portal into the cottage room.

A fall of pebbles is heard and there is a fleeting glimpse of a brown-skinned figure with a face wizened, eyes bright and horns, swept-back and curving, jutting from his head.

"'Seeker I, 'neath star-webbed sky,
Wait in shadow of th'ancient tree.
The cosmos whirls! My spirit flies!
Is this His joyous melody?"'

A naked girl can be seen running through the shadows, her laughter, with her footfalls, diminishing on their ears. Hooves clatter, seemingly in pursuit.

"'Through cypress, oak; through haunted vale
And moonlit grove His pipes resound
Ere Eos tints the mountains pale:
Great Pan is nigh but never found!"' [3]

The scene fades to nothing, to darkness.

Mr Pixum set a spill to the dying fire and carefully re-lit the lamp. Before he could speak, Mr Fox said:

'But they're nothing but imaginary worlds, wrought from the mind-stuff of creative imagination!'

'And what do you suppose any world is wrought from?' returned Mr Pixum with some venom, 'The univi are great thoughts. We're all in this together. We either create or we destroy. Some univi are nothing but a mediocre thought, some are not even that. Some univi are plain silly. Be grateful you inhabit a place of infinite wonder and mystery, beauty, grotesquerie and eeriness. The proliferation of the ubiquitous teapot motif aside,' with a glance towards the Teapot Man, 'we, thank Odin, are not in a silly universe.'

The Teapot Man pursed his lips.

'Think about it,' went on Mr Pixum, 'We create our own worlds within Worlds. Each of us affects everyone else. Think of happiness. Think of it as our "ground state." Should we deviate from it, we alone are responsible for its loss. So it is with the Eater of Worlds. Here we have the consequence of such a deviation, a misconception. It is a form of stupidity, but even so, stupidity that we can forgive because it is probably unintentional.'

Mr Pixum took a swallow from the cider flagon.

'I believe someone is very hurt and very empty. They are sucking in the Worlds, desperate to fill the void within, desperate to hit out and destroy that which it blames for its suffering. Books quicken the Worlds, without them dreams fade and die. The Eater of Worlds would fill the screaming vacuum inside itself with anything. Unfortunately nothing will give the wretched creature the peace and succour it craves but the missing piece of its essence. You have seen what is happening to the World of Pyrates. They may rollick and cavort now, but their time is running out. And so is ours!'

Mr Pixum strode to the door and flung it open.

'Come, let's attend to the business at hand!'

The three friends hurtled along the Maenporth lane leading to Falmouth. The Teapot Man felt an urge to look over his shoulder.

'There's nothing behind us!' he shouted.

'Should there be?' asked Mr Fox.

'The rest of the world should be!' replied the Teapot Man, 'But it's gone!'

His two friends glanced behind them. Sure enough, there was nothing at all.

The town of Falmouth was dull, the streets deserted. The façades of the buildings were insubstantial.

Mr Pixum brought the gig to a halt outside the bookseller's which was in an advanced state of fading away. He viewed the scene through his Magick Eye, which still had some use, albeit limited. It was as if a great whirlwind was drawing in everyone and everything from all the Worlds into its vortex; he saw that the closer to the bookshop they were, the more grainy and less solid everything became.

Oliver Probus and his fiancée, Aliya Haddaway, were huddled in the street. Mr Pixum was straight to the point.

'The focus is here! The Eater of Worlds is dining right here! What do you know about this?'

Although fright moulded his features, Oliver Probus stood up for himself.

'We've done nothing. It's nothing to do with us!'

To which he added: 'My books are crumbling!'

Mr Fox was thinking that the Pyrates could no longer be heard, but no sooner had he thought this than the Dead Pyrate appeared from out of the night, shouldered him aside, pushed open the bookseller's door and stumped upstairs. Clump, thock!

'Is there anyone else here?' asked Mr Pixum, 'Tell me now! We may be too late!'

'No one,' said the bookseller sullenly.

Aliya looked at him then quickly lowered her eyes. When she spoke to Mr Pixum, her manner was subdued.

'Elic is still upstairs, I think,' she said.

'Elic?' said Mr Pixum, 'Who is Elic?'

Oliver spoke up. 'No one important. He lodges in the room above the shop but he's nothing to concern yourself about.'

With some emotion, Aliya said: 'He's Elic Treakle. He's a dear man! He was my . . . We were to be married.'

She looked ashamed. 'Then I met Oliver and things changed.' She hung her head. 'He's kept to his room since I broke the news to him. I take him his food, but he doesn't . . .'

Without a word, Mr Pixum burst into the shop and ran upstairs. Mr Fox and the Teapot Man followed. More pyrates clambered up after them, their footsteps laggardly, drained of vigour.

Elic Treakle sat in the corner of his cheerless room, slumped in his chair. A ghastly expression desolated his features and his hair writhed as if moved by deep, undersea tides. The walls and ceiling were grainy and fading. A host of insubstantial figures gathered about his sorry form. Many were pyrates but there were others, too. Mr Pixum could see Robin Hood and—was that Little John with the quarter-staff? More and more wraiths joined the gathering. Those drawn closest to Elic Treakle, Eater of Worlds, began to elongate and slip into Elic's open mouth. Eating his own World with all the others, Elic Treakle himself began to fade along with the rest of existence.

Mr Pixum, himself now becoming translucent, rushed back downstairs to the gig and returned with a candle and a book.

'The work of my friend Mr Coleridge will be crucial if I am to succeed,' he thought, pushing through the throng to stand at Elic's elbow.

With the Worlds on the brink of oblivion, with all the creations of imagination about to vanish from existence forever, it could be said that here was a man, a pixie, upon the shoulders of whom rested the last chance to prevent this fate, this cruel and unnecessary end to Life's crowning glory.

To say Mr Pixum's hand trembled as he grasped the book would be untrue, for he understood all. With the blessings of the pixie caps glowing through his very quiddity, dissolving even the vaguest notion of girders constricting his soul, he knew his plan was precisely the course of action required and he would perform it. Certainty possessed him, he was the remedy, both lever and fulcrum, in the illusion of space and time he was the source of everything that was, is and ever will be, and he would save *everything*. He knew he was part of that creation, as are we all, and he also knew he had the power to save the Worlds: he became the moment, flowed into it.

'Elic!' he yelled, 'Hear me!'

This produced no response.

Mr Pixum slammed the book down on to the writing desk before the Eater of Worlds.

'Read!' he demanded, his voice a deep baritone.

Elic's lips quivered, shapes slithered into the black maw of his mouth.

'Read!' bellowed Mr Pixum, 'Now! With me!'

By the light of the candle, leaning over Elic's shoulder he opened the book and began to read aloud. Elic's eyes appeared to follow the words.

> *"It is an ancient Mariner,*
> *And he stoppeth one of three.*
> *By thy long grey beard and glittering eye,*
> *Now wherefore stopp'st thou me?*
> *The Bridegroom's doors are opened wide,*
> *And I am next of kin;*
> *The guests are met, the feast is set:*

May'st hear the merry din."'

Mr Pixum maintained a steady voice, unrelenting, stern. His very tone urged his companion to join in.

'"He holds him with his skinny hand,
'There was a ship,' quoth he.
'Hold off! unhand me, grey beard loon!'
Eftsoons his hand dropt he.
He holds him with his glittering eye —
The Wedding-Guest stood still,
And listens like a three years child:
The Mariner hath his will."'

And so it went, through storm, drought and ice, until (with two strong voices reading aloud)—

'"God save thee, ancient Mariner!
From the fiends that plague thee thus! —
'Why look'st thou so?'
— With my cross-bow
I shot the ALBATROSS."'

And on and on until, semi-redeemed—

'"He prayeth best, who loveth best
All things both great and small;
For the dear God who loveth us,
He made and loveth all."' [4]

Beads of sweat stood out on Mr Pixum's forehead.
The room was solid. The Dead Pyrate left the room humming a sea shanty.
For his selfishness, Elic, *"A sadder and a wiser man,"* was made to make an oath on the spot.

'Or your life is forfeit,' said Mr Pixum.

An ineffable sadness cloaking him, Long John Silver made to leave.

'Me keel's driftwood, shipmate. I seen a thing or two at sea . . . but by the powers I ain't seen the like o' this,' he said. On his shoulder, the parrot ruffled his feathers. 'An' it fair put a creak in Cap'n Flint's rudder.'

Mr Pixum touched his arm and spoke gently.

'The Summer *will* return, my friend,' he said.

The pyrate managed a grin as he left.

'I knowed that old Mariner meself. Ye're a smart lad!'

Port flowed back at the cottage.

'One could write a novel about this adventure,' said Mr Fox with exuberance, tilting his glass.

'A precise record is all that is required,' said Mr Pixum tartly, 'Neatness and pat endings we can leave for the twee fictifiers, the plagiarisers, the hacks.'

'Just a thought,' murmured the fox, rolling his eyes.

'Events appear to have given Miss Haddaway doubts about her bookseller,' said The Teapot Man, 'which may prove to be a good thing.'

'Um . . . hum,' muttered Mr Pixum, 'the Dead Pyrate thinks he can find her a position at the Curiosity Shop.'

'Poddy, old chap, this "dear god" that appears in the verse . . .' began Mr Fox contemplatively, 'Is the poet referring to any god in particular, do you know?'

'Take your pick,' Mr Pixum raised his eyebrows nonchalantly, 'It hardly matters.' He patted both hands several times on the arms of his chair. 'I would choose Pan, Odin or even Jack-in-the-Green . . . or Puck, they all fit well enough, I suppose.'

The fox thought for a moment.

'Oh, in that case I prefer Sigyn or Ran as ideals but I feel more at home with Dionysus.' He thought for another moment. 'Actually

I'll plump for Pan, the horned fox! Much more my cup of tea!'

They helped themselves to cold meats, lapsing into silence while they ate and contemplated existence, and its opposite, and inwardly sighed with relief when the port resumed it's circulation.

'A wonderful if harsh penance,' beamed Mr Fox presently, 'Henceforth, should Elic feel in the least dejected, he must flourish that very text and declaim it in its entirety to the nearest person! I, for one, will take great pains to avoid him.'

'And to complete his healing, he must hug a rowan tree!' laughed The Teapot Man. 'Where do you get these from, Pixum?'

Mr Pixum's only reply was a tired but enigmatic smirk. He had imposed the penances for their efficaciousness but had no interest in explaining that now, he was thinking about the morrow when Lucinda was due to return. He would hear her horse trotting up the track and he would step out of the cottage to greet her. She would dismount and throw her arms about him then pull away, her smile accentuating her dimples, her eyes mocking, attempting to bore into his mind, asking, 'I do hope you managed to occupy your time pleasantly while I've been away?' And he would reply in an offhand manner, his glance skimming the horizon, 'Pleasantly enough, my dear,' and with a raised eyebrow he would add, 'Though we had the odd moment when things were quite thin . . .'

A little later the Teapot Man sniggered.

'Just think of it! The Worlds nearly came to an end due to an "Elic Treakle" fault!'

Note for Sceptics: Those readers who have a credibility problem with Dead Pyrates walking about should take into account that what we take for granted as a living body consists of at least one Double or Astral Body, call it what you will, which can be projected intentionally and is often projected unintentionally. The Double is an automaton to a greater or lesser degree. How much more likely that a fictitious character can lurk, dead and dusty, for years among the detritus of a "Curiosity Shop" before it re-animates and goes its merry way? So, then, what if this entity is a combination of both of the above? Still have a problem? Quite simply, we are all wrought from mind-stuff. Try to avoid putting such strict limitations on so-called "reality"—it is always much more than meets the eye.

1. *Pirate Ditty*, Robert Louis Stevenson (1850 - 1894)
2. From *Greenwood*, Gilbert Nightingale (1787 - 1873)
3. *Hic Vivit Deo*, Percy Kensington Fernside FRS (1682 - 1776)
4. From *The Rime of the Ancient Mariner*, Samuel Taylor Coleridge (1772 - 1834)

Twice Bitten, Once Shy

Mr Pixum called a cab and rounded up his friends from their homes and carried them away to a house in the woods.

No he didn't.

It had indeed been Mr P's intention to whisk his friends off to a particular house in the woods but a message he received that morning necessitated a change of plan; a house with a collapsed roof held scant appeal. This was disappointing as the house was purported to contain a matter-transportation device constructed mainly of candles. It can be imagined that this piqued Mr Pixum's curiosity. However, he would have to attend to this matter at another time.

Since the cab was on its way to collect him, Mr Pixum decided that some sort of expedition was necessary, and he needed to acquire a replacement part for his Vayveltweem Tempyreacon,* the "Vayve" as Mr Pixum had come to call it, thus it was into the teeming bustle of London Town that he was bound.

The cab arrived.

'Where to?' asked the cabbie.

'Already am,' replied Mr Pixum, deliberately misinterpreting, 'I intend to keep warm.'

It was a chill morning bright with sunshine, the streets and rooftops still wet with dew as Mrs Enderby, Mr P's housekeeper, watched from the doorway of Mr Pixum's townhouse. A strange atmosphere pervaded the morning; the soft sunshine, the echoing sounds all about, the aroma of new growth, all combined, like an orchestra, to play an air that confidently declared the coming of spring. Waving in the light breeze, crocuses and grape hyacinths danced in the occasional pocket-sized garden and window box. The cab clattered away along the cobbled street towards the residence of, firstly The Teapot Man and secondly Mr Fox, thence into London Town.

Mr Pixum, scholar, mage, prophet and various other quietly self-inferred honorifics, marshalled his thoughts as he was carried at an uneven judder through streets of busy beings bustling about their business. He felt impelled to keep a close watch on his thoughts as he suspected that he may have been creating or erasing people and things by a series of seemingly harmless whimsies. The faulty Vayve was the secondary reason this may have come about as the device tended to amplify one's imaginings—among other things—indiscriminately, depending upon the settings. It was for the operator to bring discrimination to the table, as it were, and use the device in a responsible manner. Mr Pixum thought of himself as "not irresponsible" but reluctantly admitted to his inmost self that he was wont to indulge in the occasional bout of mental frivolity.

After the usual exchange of pleasantries, Mr Pixum, Mr Fox and The Teapot Man, the completed Feathers of Fate, rode in silence to their destination in the vicinity of Covent Garden.

'I can hear my belly rumble,' said Mr Fox, his voice inflected with a note of warning to any potential objection, 'I vote we take comestibles on board right away!'

Crowds meandered and hurried before a backdrop of haphazardly placed buildings. These edifices, exuding a powerful sense of antiquity, seemed to rear up and lean over the narrow street, almost forming a tunnel, forcing upon the observer with a great deal of emphasis, the ancient dreams and memories inherent in the quiet piles of stone. Hanging signs representing teapots of various shapes and sizes indicated a sprinkling of tearooms and, a short way down on their left, was an eating house named "Pollard's" which looked respectable enough. A fresh coat of paint in dark green gloss gave the establishment the air of having an inflated opinion of itself.

'"Meals now being served,"' said Mr Fox, reading a placard leaning against the frontage, '"A Guinea Per Head."' A trifle steep don't you think?'

'"R.O.B. Twelve Guineas,"' read The Teapot Man, 'What on Earth can that mean?'

Mr Pixum pushed open the door, wrinkled his nose at the unusual aroma, and peered within, almost immediately turning back to his friends, a strange expression upon his features.

'"Rest Of Body,"' he said.

'I see,' said Mr Fox.

'I don't think you do, Bertie,' replied Mr Pixum, 'take a look for yourself.'

He moved aside to allow the other two an unobstructed view of the murky interior.

'*Metis, apportez votre seau!*' exclaimed Mr Fox.

Diners' heads perched upon the kind of supports that held cocoa-nuts on fairground shies and were engaged in tugging place-mats with their teeth (as much as they could) until the platter was close enough for them to snag a morsel. By some quirk or humourous intent, many items on the menu consisted of "canapés." Some of the "per head"s had managed to roll on to their platters, the better to consume their meals while they were still hot, blisters forming as they wallowed in the boiling gravy. They adopted a sort of "cheek and jaw shuffle" to manoeuvre around.

Along one wall the "R.O.B"s hung by their coat collars from a row of stout pegs; mercifully hats were hung to cover the unencumbered necks.

'What on Earth are you serving in here?' asked Mr Pixum, clearly astounded, of the maitre d', who ceased to clean his fingernails with a dining fork and looked up in anticipation at the three staring faces.

With a nonchalant shrug he replied, 'Old apples, old onions, old potatoes, old mutton, old sweetbreads, anything we can find in the gutter really. Are you eating here or what?'

'No, I think we'll leave it today, thank you' said Mr Pixum.

'Don't be so hasty,' replied the maitre d', 'You don't have to dine among these tight-fisted skinflints. Why, for a mere thirteen guineas each you can sit up in chairs and feed yourselves by hand! It pains me to serve quality fare for a pittance but it gives me much pleasure to show off the chef's culinary skills to such obviously discerning gentlefolk as yourselves.'

'Despite your persuasive arguments, my reluctance still holds good,' said Mr Pixum, closing the door, 'I bid you good day.'

'Suit yourselves,' murmured the maitre d' off-handedly, 'It's your loss.'

Bowls of steaming stew accompanied by hunks of bread purchased from a street vendor proved a satisfactory alternative to "eating in" for the three friends and they set off with Mr Pixum leading the way through a maze of streets and courtyards.

'As I think of the World, so it becomes,' muttered Mr Pixum.

'What was that you said?' asked The Teapot Man.

'Thinking aloud,' said Mr Pixum.

'I fancy that establishment yonder,' said Mr Fox, 'The very place to quaff some ale, it seems to me!'

The Teapot Man rolled a glassy eye towards his companion.

'My friend, you are always giving in to your desires. Eating this, quaffing that! It will do you good to just *be* for once!'

'Tosh! If we were not meant to quaff, we would imbibe from hour-glasses!'

'There may be time enough tomorrow for a little indulgence,' said Mr Pixum, 'It's only an hour or so away and I would like to collect the replacement part for the Vayve before we are distracted by anything else.'

Mr Pixum *was* distracted for a second by the sight of Mr Fox handing some coins to a wayside waif and, when he looked up, a tableau of pathetic aspect appeared before him.

A roly-poly couple were sitting dejectedly upon some luggage in the street. They both had faces resembling, in proportion, the full moon, together with an assortment of chins. The lady whose face, Mr Pixum easily deduced, was normally very pretty, wept into a large kerchief, emotion transforming her features into a cartwheel of misery.

Instantly recognising this unfortunate family as the subject of the message he had earlier received, Mr Pixum understood why his source had chosen to inform him. The message had been brief: "Large family in Henrietta Street, Covent Garden, destitute. Victims of cheating."

Also struck by this array of melancholy, Mr Fox stepped forward and enquired.

'Pray excuse me, sir, may I delve into the origin of your obvious trouble?'

'Forgive us this embarrassing display of misery, sir, for we have most recently been struck such a blow from which I fear we shall not recover—and 'tis all my own doing!'

The man struggled to his feet and bowed.

'Mr L E Fant at your service, sir, and this is my darling wife, Ellie.'

He helped the lachrymose woman to her feet in as gainly a manner as was possible.

'And these,' asked Mr Pixum, stepping up and sweeping his hand in a gesture that took in five or six porky children lolling on the ground in various attitudes of apathy, 'are your little jumbos?'

This acted upon Mrs Fant as a reminder of the difficulty of providing for so many hungry wet mouths and the stricken creature quivered herself into an even greater fit of sobbing, a sight to melt the hardest of hearts.

Mr Pixum, his mouth set in a firm line, nodded towards a nearby tavern by the name of The Feline Fox, ('A name,' thought Mr Fox with a smile, 'that reminds me of an erstwhile amour') and to Mr Fant, he said: 'Bring your family inside, sir. We'll help you with your trunks and then we'll treat all of you to refreshments while you relate to us your tale of woe.'

The Fants, all smutched breeches, soiled silks and stained waistcoats, were allowed to settle by a fire of truly Luciferian embers and feed on gargantuan amounts of pie before Mr L E Fant, with a sleeve, wiped the grease from his mouth and unfolded his tale.

'I am truly ashamed to admit that I have a weakness for speculation, gentlemen,' he began, 'and fell foul of a notorious swindler (I didn't know that at the time), one Gordon Knowm. It happened in the following manner...'

Mr Fant went on to tell of a blooming friendship (as he thought) based upon their common interest in "the fancy" or the "sport" of pugilism, a friendship initiated by Knowm, which led to Fant, being encouraged by his new friend, to wager ever greater amounts of money on a succession of prizefights, all of which brought him jackpot winnings. Then came the last boxing match. Assured by Knowm that he was on to a certain winner—"'Inside information. Know what I mean?'" (a finger tapping the side of his nose)—Fant placed not only all of his cash but also the freehold of his house and all of his belongings on the contest. 'A little rash, admittedly.' Mr Fant had attended few of these bouts, and when the day of this major fight came, he was unable to be there either, owing to a sudden illness which struck him down the morning after he had been treated to dinner by his friend, Gordon Knowm.

And Knowm, it transpired, was a bookmaker.

'I own I was rather slow to catch on,' said Fant.

'The fight was between twins: The Shoreditch Hammer and The Shoreditch Anvil,' Mr Fant continued, 'and Knowm assured me they were well-known to "the fancy." As advised, I put everything on The Anvil. I expected to become a rich man.'

'What went wrong?' asked The Teapot Man.

'Gordon came to our house after the fight and informed me that we'd lost everything. My heart died in my breast. I was destroyed. Knowm was not in the least sympathetic. He said it was a gamble, admittedly a supposedly rigged gamble, but a gamble nonetheless. It was too bad. *Too bad?* I had to do something! I went to a tavern close to the venue where the fight took place, spoke to some disgruntled gamblers and discovered the truth.'

'Which was. . .?' asked Mr Pixum, impatiently.

Mr Fant's eyes twinkled with tears; his wife released a moan of despair and resumed her weeping.

'The Shoreditch Hammer and The Shoreditch Anvil are Siamese twins.'

'*Siamese twins?*' Mr Pixum was aghast.

'Aye, joined at the neck.'

'Joined at the *neck?*'

'Joined at the neck and sharing one head.'

'*One head?*'

Mr Fant nodded his great lunar head.

'One head with two brains.'

'Two br—'

'One head, two brains, two bodies, four fists.'

Mr Fant folded his arms, rested them upon his ample convexity and pouted his lower lip. One of the jumbos broke wind, setting off a wave of giggles that rippled across the spongy mound of offspring.

'I suspect foul play,' said Mr Pixum.

Mr Fant continued.

'They went at each other like hammer and tongs.'

'Ham and tongue,' said Mr Fox thoughtfully rubbing his waistcoat, 'would go down very well right now.'

Mr Fant resumed.

'After the knockout, the twins were revived by the usual bucket of water. When asked who knocked out whom they each claimed to be the winner. Gordon Knowm was seen to have a quiet word with them. Shortly after that the fight was decided in favour of The Hammer.'

'When Nature cuts corners and men take advantage of the fact,' stated Mr Pixum, 'all manner of trouble ensues.'

Mr Pixum lit his pipe, a faraway gaze in his eye.

'Obviously the fight was rigged,' he concluded.

Mr Fox, eyebrows raised, glanced at The Teapot Man who rolled *his* eyes.

'Astounding powers of deduction,' said he.

Unfazed, Mr Pixum pursued his train of thought.

'The twins receive the purse whichever of them is the winner but I suspect they were advised to declare in favour of the twin who took the least bets, thus enlarging Knowm's takings, in return for a share of the said takings to add to "their" purse.'

'Then Knowm gets away with it?' asked The Teapot Man.

'In the customary practice, certainly,' replied Mr Pixum, 'We'll never prove any misdeed. If people are foolish enough to gamble, they have to accept the outcome.'

He paused. 'Although in the case of the Fants I think we should arrange for some form of redress.'

Mr Pixum's sense of being in some way responsible for this whole calamity finally hit home. He had noticed, as the tale was related, Mr Fant's hand flicker and become, briefly, a leg of chicken; Ellie Fant's head had shimmered into a very life-like stilton cheese before resuming its pretty, miserable countenance and the juvenile jumbos had flickered and popped in and out of being an assortment of pies and sticky buns.

Also, worryingly, tendrils of smoke had emitted from Mr Fant's nose (Mr Pixum's first thought was "trunk"; his second thought was "pipe", both of which he hastily dismissed), bearing the very aroma of his favourite perique tobacco. He was almost convinced that he was their creator, having manifested them as part of a pre-prandial whimsy. Whether or not this was indeed factual—and there was more, and stranger, evidence now that he came to contemplate it, albeit circumstantial, that concerned the whole "Pollards" episode: the maitre d' having distinctive arachnid qualities in spite of the fact that Mr P always thought of spiders as female even though he knew very well that they came in both sexes most of the time, which reminded him of another whimsy inspired by an encounter in his privy: he walked right into a large web strung across the doorway resulting in its shockingly hefty occupant being deposited upon his nose, and in his surprise he'd batted the eight-legged bounder straight into the earth-closet . . . He was, all the same, moved to help the poor Fants. Whether or not the defective Vayve had amplified his whimsies and made them flesh was neither here nor there.

Having installed the Fants at the nearby Inn of The Whey-Faced Monkey, the three friends continued on Mr Pixum's errand. Tuesday morning had passed into Wednesday afternoon over two hours ago: the diurnal calendar having recently been adjusted so that the days changed at midday instead of at midnight: this was possibly an idea thought up by the Lord Mayor of London to keep Londoners "on their toes" or probably another caprice of Mr Pixum's unconscious. The afternoon sky was already beginning to lose its bright disposition. Mr Fox bought them all roasted chicken legs from a stall and they ate as they walked.

Mr Pixum remained uncomfortable.

'This is unbelievable. It all sounds like an elaborate and ridiculous fantasy. You couldn't make this up if you tried!'

'The Shoreditch twins are surely a peculiarity—or peculiari-*ties*—in the world of pugilism?' said The Teapot Man, 'Though I doubt that would furrow the brow of any gambler. . .'

'Swindling is embedded in gambling and gamblers are prone to fool themselves as much as they're fooled by the crooks,' commented Mr Fox.

'A more thrifty method of delivering your statement,' said The Teapot Man, 'would have been to introduce into it the adjective, "gullible" early on and leave it at that . . .'

Foplets' tiny emporium was found in a suitably small cul-de-sac, sandwiched between a bakery and a cheese shop.

Mr Pixum, Mr Fox and The Teapot Man crammed themselves inside. Light from a lantern hanging from a ceiling beam limned shelves upon which boxes and jars, eggs, teapots, tripods, dried fungi, kippers, valves, wishers, washers, astrolabes and convolvuli jostled for space. In one corner nestled a nest of periodic tables. In short, it was cluttered.

The proprietor, Drog Foplets, greeted Mr Pixum warmly as an old and valued customer and sniffled and wiped a nose rubicund with wear and tear. Mr Pixum stated his business, whereupon Mr Foplets proceeded to rearrange almost two thirds of the items in the shop, displacing enough dust to have them all sneezing violently, before he located the item. As he unwrapped it from a square of oilcloth they saw it was a small and intricate contrivance consisting mainly of polished brass and rubies.

'There we are, Mr P. Once you replace the old part with this beauty, your old Vayveltweem will be as right as railings. Earth, air, fire and water all synchronised and limit-checked.'

The Teapot Man peered closely at the gleaming item.

'Is this some sort of governor?' he asked.

'Elemental, my dear Teapot Man' replied Mr Πixum.

⋙ ✦ ⋘

'We'll meet in an hour's time,' said Mr Pixum as he and The Teapot Man headed off to visit a bookseller in a nearby court. Mr Fox had an urge to stretch his legs by strolling the streets, his comfortable top boots added pleasure to such a jaunt; he wanted to move at his own somewhat speedier pace and to please himself for a while, taking in his surroundings. He made his way to Bloomsbury via Holborn with no conscious intent. As he turned out of a side street on to the Square he overheard a woman say, 'Mind yerself, yer in me vision. I can't see!'

'See what?' asked the fox.

'*Who*, you mean! Who!'

'Well, who then?'

'Ella Dessai, large as lice, paradin' parst yer nose on the arm o' that puffed up ol' toad!'

Mr Fox looked. The fur on his neck bristled.

The name was familiar. Of course it was! "Ella Dessai" was an alias (or "nom de swindler," he thought) of Vinnie Bentley, to use his "town name," or one of them, the same Bentley the Feathers of Fate had delivered up to a very particular judgement some time ago. There had to be another "Ella Dessai." It *couldn't* be Bentley after all. All the same, his curiosity insisted he at least have a look.

The street was crowded and the pavement had become quite thick with bystanders. Bertie Fox had to fight his way forward in order to see anything. In the way of gawpers they had clotted together and formed a wall of backs. He found a gap eventually and peered through it.

He never had discarded the unease he had felt about the Bentley situation . . . but this was someone else, surely? Had The Teapot Man made an error? Could face powder disguise the flagrant arrogance, the boorishness that oozed from every tedious plane of Bentley's features? Was Ella Dessai a separate individual entirely? He didn't recall The Teapot Man saying he had set eyes upon this incarnation of the murthering cheat but had "made enquiries" or something to that effect. Or had an opportunist jumped into Dessai's slippers in order to take advantage of her reputation, dubious as it was? He had not discussed his disquiet with his friends. Bentley certainly deserved punishment for his crimes and his removal from society was for the common good but the manner in which this had been performed left a cold rat in the pit of his stomach when he thought about it.

The couple was now no more than a couple of yards away. They were indeed "parading;" Dessai's companion resembled a penguin, more portly Beau Nash than toad (forgiving himself the mixed zoology), though he strolled the stroll of overweening self-congratulation. The jewelled and lace bedecked trollop on his arm wore a visage as white as bone china, a small black heart adorned her upper lip and a beauty patch of purple velvet was glued to her cerused cheek. Even with a hogsworth of blanc plastered over it, thought the fox, this was definitely not the face of Bentley. He had to discover more.

A retinue of what had to be sycophants made up the procession. He slipped into the line and sauntered along with them. Inane conversation fluttered from fop to spark to fop but after several minutes he gleaned nothing more than a few irrelevant fashion tips and some salacious gossip concerning personages of whom he had never heard.

Aware that his rendezvous required him to return to Covent Garden shortly, Mr Fox took a chance.

'Are nuptials in the offing?' he asked of a nearby dandy. It was a wild guess.

'Oh hah hah! What a thing to ask!' Eyes rolled up, he looked down his nose. 'Ev'ry body knows! Why, you must have come directly from the Indies. Hah hah!'

'It is true I have been in Town for only a short while,' Mr Fox said in as gentle a voice as he could manage, 'My visit has been taken up with various time-consuming matters thus depriving me of the latest news. I am become so dull. Pray tell me something of interest, I beg you.'

'You must have heard, sirrah! Matrimony *is* in the offing! Engagement is the order of this day.'

'The party is en route to celebrate?'

'Gad, sir! You are as sharp as a dart! We go to celebrate the event as I speak! It is held at Jessie's, she is our kind hostess!'

'Jessie's?'

'Lady Jessie Nobile, *la belle dame* of Bloomsbury! My, you have been preoccupied for an *age*!'

Mr Fox met his friends on the hour, out of breath and hot as a freshly boiled pudding.

❧ ✣ ☙

It was very late when they returned to Mr Pixum's home, the fox and The Teapot Man having been invited to stay the night for practical purposes; Wednesday afternoon had long become Wednesday morning. The new part had been successfully installed in the Vayve, Bertie had informed Mr Pixum and The Teapot Man of his Bloomsbury news, Mrs Enderby had aired the bedding in the spare rooms and all three friends were ready to turn in for the night.

'Before we retire,' said The Teapot Man to Mr Pixum, 'I wonder whether you will satisfy my curiosity?'

'I'll do my best' replied Mr Pixum.

'How do you plan to return this miscreant Gordon Knowm's ill-gotten gains to the Fants?'

'By as direct a means as possible,' replied Mr Pixum, 'for we have here a foe of inferior qualities and seemingly no redeeming features. A low man. A petty crook. A swindler.'

The Teapot Man knocked out his pipe in the fireplace, straightened up and leaned forward, his knuckles on the tabletop.

'I think this swindler needs teaching a particular kind of lesson,' he said, 'I have an idea for just that, an entrée, if you like. And swift action is also required in the case of our wayward "Bentley."'

The Feathers of Fate were up and about their business at first light. Mr Fox searched out an old friend who made it his business to know the insalubrious details of all those duckers, dippers and swervers that contaminated the capital, no matter from what social rank.

Mr Pixum and The Teapot Man paid a visit to Lady Jessalin Nobile but were sent away for being too early. This little setback enabled them to break their fast in proper fashion at an eating house a few streets away. When her ladyship finally dragged herself from her slumbers, the previous night's excitement having quite worn her out, they were received semi-graciously into her salon which yet reeked of sweat and tobacco, the jollity having concluded all too recently. Lady Jessalin gave them the information for which they sought in exchange for Mr Pixum's promise to be at her service on one occasion in the future, should she ever be in need of it.

They found Kippy Brimacombe at his address by Grosvenor Square given to them by Lady Jessalin Nobile. Knowing these well-apportioned rooms were part of the sham he used to beguile his wealthy victims, Mr Pixum wasted no time on manners and niceties, he came straight out with his findings.

Brimacombe, his behaviour initially most spirited, gradually deflated, moving from his heroic pose by the marble fireplace to slumping upon a nearby chair, chins overhanging his stock, belly bloated. The exposure of Dessai to be one and the same Vinnie Bentley, a name he had heard associated with unseemly goings-on, left him sagging in his finery, the very picture of bewilderment and embarrassment. He sat with his head in his hands and moaned.

Surprisingly, after not too many minutes had elapsed, he pulled himself up, drew in his paunch and spoke.

'I heard a rumour about Bentley,' he said, as if Bentley and Dessai were separate entities, 'Lady Jessalin passed it on to me. He'd been attacked and robbed of something priceless. He said he knew his attacker. Someone else of whom I have heard no good.'

'His name, if you please.'

'Teddy Chosque. A rum cove.'

'And your liaison with Ella Dessai?'

'A nod and a wink, that's all it took. I'm ashamed to say I was captured even as I was playing her at her own game.'

His features, at first pale and drooping, ripened into a tomato hue. *Over*-ripened, thought Mr Pixum.

'Him? *Him!* I must have honour!'

'Shall I ring for a glass of something?' asked Mr Pixum.

'Not necessary, not . . . necessary,' replied Brimacombe, 'I shall be fully myself presently.'

Kippy Brimacombe forced himself to his feet and gazed out of the window.

'Y'know it's a strange thing to have such knowledge, to realise the dream is vanquished at one stroke. Ah, but the tease is invariably better than the act . . . But I'll tell you, this new vision of what now *is* cannot level the anticipation already relished, not a bit of it!'

'Have you a plan, Mr Brimacombe? Will you walk away or . . ?'

Brimacombe, his breath wheezing and rapid, looked Mr Pixum in the eye.

'Walk away? I shall not! I shall have satisfaction! Nothing else is creditable. No apologies printed in *The Grub-Street Journal*! Leave it to me, I shall send my man to Bentley. Pistols, sirs! You have my gratitude—though you have stripped me naked before my peers. Now leave me. I require some moments of reflection.'

Mr Fox joined Mr Pixum and The Teapot Man, meeting them at the same eating house they had adjourned to only an hour and a half previously. The fox tucked into a plate of mutton chops while the other two took only a pot of tea.

'Ella Dessai can *only* be Bentley,' said the fox, wiping gravy from his muzzle, 'Dorwart has word of the man's presence in various locations about Town, also Ella Dessai is sailing proudly through the top levels of Society and is much feted . . . *Blood and 'ounds!* I don't understand this at all. I spent long enough with the man to recognise his turpitudinous fizzog anywhere. It ain't him.'

There was no surprise upon Mr Pixum's forthright features as he listened.

'We now know—or we're all but certain we know—that the man you entertained in East Anglia was not Bentley,' he said, 'and, with the same quality of certainty, we also know whom he really was.'

The chop Mr Fox was about to bite into was paused within an inch of oblivion. Pouring more tea for The Teapot Man and himself, Mr Pixum resumed.

'Like many a vagabond, our imposter could not refrain from bragging about his schemes. Someone he confided in, someone he had insisted must swear an oath never to reveal this secret to anyone at all, told someone else and so it was passed on until it reached the ear of a gentleman with whom we have but recently conversed.'

'And this was . . ?'

'Ella Dessai's betrothed, the "toad" or "penguin" as you described him, one Kippy Brimacombe. He's a wealthy man by all accounts—except one.'

'Which is . . ?'

'The true one. You see, Brimacombe practices the same "trade" as Bentley.'

'Birds of the same feather,' said The Teapot Man.

'You mean each was fooled by the other's dissimulation?'

Bertie Fox took a gulp from his tankard to prevent himself from choking. He wiped his eyes with his napkin.

'Come on then! My imposter was . . ?'

Gordon Knowm flew backwards into his malodorous hallway, tripped over his flea-ridden hound and landed on his backside. Mr Pixum had decided to beard the crook in his crib.

'We've come to collect all the money, title deeds and everything else you cheated out of the Fants,' said Mr Pixum, 'Now hand over everything forthwith!'

Knowm, rising slowly to his feet, eyed the door at the end of the hall.

'Don't even think of making a run for the back door,' said Mr Pixum, 'It's guarded.'

Knowm, a squat man with a fringe of beard around his face, looked affronted. The hound cringed at his feet.

'I am no cheat,' he said, 'Fant lost his bet. There's an end of it. It was all fair and square.'

'Fair?' exploded Mr Pixum, 'What would you know about fair? You are a liar and a scoundrel!'

'You can't prove it!' said Knowm with a sneer, 'So take yourself off before I set the dog on you!'

'We'll leave here when we get what we came for,' said Mr Pixum.

'I couldn't give you anything back even if I wanted to,' said Knowm gleefully, 'My angle is angling. I've liquidated all my assets by changing them into fish!'

'Fish?' said The Teapot Man incredulously, coming out from behind Mr Pixum.

'Why not?' said Knowm, 'It's a sound investment. As everybody knows, fish swim in currentsy and minnows grow into great big whales!'

'Then,' said Mr Pixum, 'I'll take you to the Bank of the River with a fishing rod!'

'What's the matter?' asked The Teapot Man.

Mr Pixum slapped his forehead. 'I can't believe *anyone* would try on that reeking tale!'

He drew his pistol.

'Hand over your loot!' he demanded, 'Now, you weasel!'

Knowm leapt at Mr Pixum. Mr Pixum fired his pistol, the shot ripped through the blowsy part of Knowm's coat sleeve. Knowm pushed past him and escaped into the street, the yelping mutt at his heels. He was unaware that, as he'd passed him in the hallway, Mr Pixum had slipped half a polished pebble into his pocket.

The Teapot Man was first to his feet and helped Mr Pixum to his. Tucking his pistol back into his belt, Mr Pixum said, 'It looks as though you, at least, Teapot Man, will have your trip to the house in the woods. Roof or no roof, let us hope those candles are working.'

Dusk was gathering when The Teapot Man stood within the circle of candles. At his feet magnetised spheres of stone rolled about a complex path of grooves chiselled out of a granite slab, a dome-shaped pebble in the centre. There was half a roof on the old house, making Mr Pixum in both ways right. The whole edifice was covered in moss as green as velvet, inside and out: it was being absorbed into the woodland, and, thought The Teapot Man, I'll allow it's much better, aesthetically, for that.

With a cab waiting, Mr Pixum dashed into his house and set the Vayve, checked the level of ground abscontius.

'Time for the *deus ex machina*,' he said to the empty room before hurrying out once more.

A cone of blue light formed above the half pebble as The Teapot Man watched; the odour of unwashed clothes and seafood seeped into the room, obliterating the elegant exhalations of Nature effecting its métier.

A thief by the name of Gordon Knowm was skulking by a whelk stall when a cone of blue light surrounded him. The next second he was gone.

The Teapot Man was ready. Even so, he was bowled over by the sudden presence of a squat body. He quickly recovered. Slipping a sack over its head, he bundled it, with significant help from the well-tipped driver, into the waiting carriage and set off to set up a reoccurrance. The candles were now pools of tallow.

Gordon Knowm flew backwards into his malodorous hallway, tripped over his flea-ridden hound and landed on his backside. Mr Pixum had decided to beard the crook in his crib.

'We've come to collect all the money, title deeds and everything else you cheated out of the Fants,' said Mr Pixum, 'Now hand over everything forthwith!'

Knowm, rising slowly to his feet, eyed the door at the end of the hall.

'Don't even think of making a run for the back door,' said Mr Pixum, 'It's guarded.'

Knowm, a squat man with a fringe of beard around his face, looked affronted. The hound cringed at his feet.

'I am no cheat,' he said, 'Fant lost his bet. There's an end of it. It was all fair and square.'

There was a thud. Gordon Knowm dropped to the floor.

Behind him, nonchalantly twirling his silver-topped cane, stood the stealthy Mr Fox.

'Sometimes one needs a second bite of the cherry,' said Mr Pixum, 'in this instance most effectively provided by the Vayve.'

The Feathers of Fate were kept very busy for the next several days. Affidavits were acquired from victims of Kippy Brimacombe and Vinnie "Ella Dessai" Bentley—those that could be persuaded to make sworn statements, at any rate—but there were more than enough, likewise in the case of Gordon Knowm.

The location and date of the duel between Brimacombe and Bentley had been winkled out of Bertie Fox's Dorwart and the other usual informants. The fox had also set a little scheme in motion with a vixen friend of his, inspired by, and with help from, Mr Pixum.

Justice John Fielding at Bow Street had been informed of all matters and was in receipt of the collection of documents. Knowm was immediately arrested and placed in a cell awaiting trial.

All that remained was for three of Fielding's constables to take their places in Hyde Park at dawn on "the day in question," Fielding having been convinced by Mr Pixum that it would be sensible to arrest Brimacombe and Bentley for duelling in the event either one of them turned slippery with the help of a canny lawyer. And duelling was a capital offence.

The dell was misty, the Seconds duly arrived with their Principals and a doctor. No birds sang. The only sound to break the silence of dawn was the muffled rumble of a cart somewhere in the distance. Lots were drawn to decide who would take the higher ground, though this was hardly necessary as the land inclined so fractionally that it looked to the naked eye to be even. There was no wind nor sunlight to bicker about, nothing more to hinder proceedings.

The Principals both wore black coats over white shirts, no blazes of colour or bright buttons, in short: nothing to distract the eye when firing.

Last minute arguments and exhortations were delivered by the Seconds. Pistols were removed from the case, examined and declared satisfactory. The Principals chose and loaded their weapons.

Brimacombe had on his face a grim, resigned expression though no trace of fear. Bentley was shaking, his eyes wild, starting from his head. The firing positions were paced out and witnessed, both parties had managed to salute each other, as was customary for evidencing a measure of civilised behaviour.

Such was the tragic scene.

Hidden by the mist, Mr Pixum, Mr Fox and the Teapot Man stood in silence beneath some trees. From their vantage point they could make out the shapes of the three constables. Moisture dripped steadily from dew-drenched leaves as if tolling the seconds.

The Seconds announced that the dropping of a kerchief would be the signal to fire.

The kerchief was dropped.

The Principals fired simultaneously.

What happened next was unexpected by the duellists, their Seconds, the doctor and the constables.

'Now that the Fants have been restored to their former state, as well as giving scores of undeserving wastrels their stake money back, I'd like to know just how the Vayveltweem and that other thing in the house in the woods actually work,' said Mr Fox, sipping his brandy, 'and so would The Teapot Man I should think.'

It was now Tuesday afternoon in The Feline Fox and would soon be Tuesday morning; it had been a long day after an even longer few days. An enfolding purple twilight gave the impression of great, soft swathes of velvet gathered among trees and catching-corners of hoary stone buildings while high above, in the west, the dome of the sky still glowed a deep sea-green, which, Mr Pixum's senses told him, keened with an ethereal plain chant as it rolled slowly—very slowly—away, following the now invisible orb of Sol. There was a breath of excitement and mizzle in the night air.

'A healthy curiosity is a good thing, my friend,' murmured Mr Pixum. 'As for The Teapot Man, there's hardly anything I can tell him that he doesn't already know, though he often feigns uninformity, as you know.'

The Teapot Man became an enigmatic smile.

'However,' said Mr Pixum, 'it's all down to energy. Easily explained. With the Vayve and whatnot, we work in symphysis from where time is turned turtle in the torque of the tides and strings of entanglement obviate the necessity of rides. See what you see, hear what you hear—use all of your senses, beauty, joy, wonder, ecstasy—all are inherent in the pure teleology of events pouring into existence, pulled forth and forged by the white heat of true will.'

Mr Pixum paused for a moment while he scratched behind his ear.

'Oh yes, the gods allow us to walk with them occasionally, once our personal vibrations acquire a certain finesse.'

Mr Fox blinked hard and let out a long sigh.

'D'you think Knowm will learn his lesson?' asked the Teapot Man, living up to feigned uninformity . . . or rhetoricality.

There was a shock. The bangs came a split second later.

Space expanded and contracted so rapidly it was next to impossible to put the experience into words. Those present witnessed something they would never forget for the rest of their lives.

The area where the duellists stood was enveloped in a glow as black as ink. Then the blackness, with instant effect, swallowed up everything.

Heads more drowning than swimming, the spectators saw the world re-emerge from nothingness, the duellists reappeared, both of whom now stood dressed only in funeral shrouds, their flesh and sinew stripped away to show bones the colour of old ivory. Their arms were straight, their pistols remained levelled at each other. From the pistols emanated sparkles of many-coloured light that scintillated into shapes and the shapes wove around them both, forming cocoons of spider-like explosions that, at first red, played through a part of the spectrum and arrived at buttercup yellow that emanated warmth and goodwill, paused for a second as if to make a point, then became sheer white brilliance that, for a few moments, blinded the onlookers. No one had noticed that the spectacle poured and swelled forth with night as it's backdrop.

An eerie whistle seethed as sparkles spat from the two figures and transformed into moving shapes: here a dragon of gold, there a full-frocked dowager in blue: a scream of agony escaped from her open mouth; a palatial edifice rose from the ground to a chorus of whistles and collapsed into fiery dust to an unearthly tune made by staccato squeakles; a man of shimmering green placed a noose around his neck and hung in the air, swaying slowly before changing into a coiling serpent of silver with eyes of ruby fire; a young maid with lank hair surrounded by a violet aura, her hands covering her face, gave a low-pitched moan that swirled around the dell. Now came a mandala of chrysanthemums and grid-like crossettes followed by a diadem of four stars that exploded into fish that swam away to fizzing sounds and then, in a cacophony of bangs, crackles and whistles, a ring exploded and in its centre grew a red teapot of at least twenty feet in width that stayed floating in the air as all sounds ceased and which then gradually diminished in size until it was a tiny point of red light. Then it winked out.

Grey light flowed back into dawn's demesne.

The constables rushed from their hiding places. Bentley and Brimacombe lay supine on the damp grass, their mortal clay and apparel restored. Mr Pixum approached the scene immediately behind the constables.

'Let them be!' he said. He waved the men away and surveyed the two duellists.

'Wake up gentlemen,' he said, 'Your lives begin anew!'

Bentley and Brimacombe blinked, looked about them . . . and smiled.

⚜

'Knowm will sort himself out in time,' replied Mr Pixum, knowing a reply was unnecessary, 'Never doubt that.'

The Teapot Man grinned and said, 'Brimacombe and Bentley have certainly learned theirs. They're now innocent as lambs.'

'Is it true,' asked Bertie Fox, 'that Knowm was taken from his cell and treated to a "Guinea Per Head" supper? Well, I hope it is. As for all three sorting themselves out, I'll believe *that* when I see it. And I *did* enjoy the fireworks.'

'Bertie, you need not doubt any of them, they have now ceased to do harm, I guarantee it. By the way, Edie made the show go with a bang; she really is a master of pyrotechny. How she contrived to include her ingredients and my small additions into the powder and shot was ingenious.'

'No jury will convict two men defending their honour, for that's how they will see it, even though neither of them possessed a grain of it,' said The Teapot Man, 'And I'm curious: the fireworks and . . . things?'

'Fire with fire. Duelling pistols for jewels of fire; they each were vain about their appearance, their looks. I infused them with *lux*. There you have the bare bones of it.'

Mr Pixum shrugged.

'It all smacks of alchemy to me . . . also something of greater pungency,' said Mr Fox, 'Well, whatever concatenation of wiles went into it, I think those scoundrels should count themselves lucky. Yes, very fortunate indeed.' He drained his brandy.

'Teddy Chorsque on the other hand . . .'

Mr Pixum put a spill to his pipe.

*See *A Fool's Errant*. Mr Pixum, after initially deciding he didn't need the device, bought it all the same. Apart from his obvious interest in its complexities, he also enjoys it as a "thing-in-itself."

Let Every Eye Negotiate

A thick bank of cloud had crept out of the north, shrouding the blue of the firmament with its pale leaden underbelly, turning what had begun as a sunny afternoon into a dull and cold one. Winter was rising out of forest and field, pushing aside the last dregs of autumn.

'Rain,' said Mr Pixum, 'can be soothing and cleansing but it can also wash away roots and drip through your ceiling.'

'But—' began Mr Fox.

'I haven't yet finished speaking,' said Mr Pixum with emphasis, giving his friend a sharp look from beneath his brows. As they made their way he continued . . .

'Rain can appear as wistful romantic longing; rain can be experienced as the sky weeping—though in its tears there is no salt—and it can make us feel cosy when we are indoors, a log fire flickering its light about the bookshelves, listening to the pattering against the panes; it reveals our reflections in puddles—and our thoughts—and it chuckles from the spouts of gargoyles. And it can soak us to the skin, making our clothing heavy and difficult to manoeuvre.'

Mr Pixum raised his eye to the lowering sky out of which snow had begun to fall.

Tilting his head to one side and rolling his eyes for the benefit of The Teapot Man, Mr Fox commented. 'What an awkward admixture; you juxtapose the subjective and the objective as if they are indistinguishable.'

He too gazed at the heaviness far above, his fur a magnificent red against the draining light's blue haze. 'And why you must go on about rain as we pass through the beauty of this friable swirling I cannot fathom.'

'Snow or rain, Bertie, it's all water.'

'They are different as chalk and calcite,' said the fox, 'To begin with, one is translucent, the other is white. Sedimentary my dear Pixum.'

Mr Pixum held out his hand, passively awaiting a snowflake to alight upon his palm.

'The difference,' he said, 'is their respective temperature.' A solitary flake landed and immediately became translucent. 'We decide for ourselves how we see things.'

'You appear to be attempting to douse this wonderful winter scene with cold water,' said Mr Fox, 'which surprises me somewhat as I have ever taken you to be something of an aesthete. I am confounded, I admit it.'

'I was making an observation,' said Mr Pixum, 'Would it please you were I to say the trees are transformed into fantastic creatures, all of them sporting a bizarre and diverse collection of white hats?'

He was about to indulge in further cogitative meanderings in his habitual tone of subtle yet heavy-footed pedantic needling when the snowball hit him fulsomely square in the face.

Mr Fox dusted off his hands. The Teapot Man was silent. Snow, with seemingly undue haste, was coming down heavily and the wind picked up, whipping the flakes into eddies. Without a word Mr Pixum wiped the snow from his cheeks and trudged on.

He was only mildly irked by this incursion into his dignity, he was more concerned with the matter at hand. They had managed to travel by coach to the village of Ristholme on the edge of Kilver Forest in the far north of England but after a pleasant night at the Gogwhistle Inn they were unable to find coach nor carriage to convey them the extra three leagues to Groque Cat Hall where they were to attend the marriage feast of Quin, the daughter of Mr Pixum's friend, Humphrey Harper, to some upstanding local. Harper had arranged for the three Feathers of Fate to be collected from the Gogwhistle Inn, though by mid-afternoon the coach still hadn't arrived. Flackman, the Inn's landlord, told them he'd heard two days ago that the snow was much heavier north of the hills though only a relatively short distance away. This morning he'd heard the storm was heading south.

'The Hall would never send a coach in this weather,' he told them, 'It would be wise to stay here and wait it out.'

Hence the cross country trek. Night was falling and the weather was downright threatening. They had decided to leave their luggage at the inn: it would not be possible to carry it across country.

They followed a course to the north-east, the sky ahead dimming rapidly whilst on the western horizon the setting sun was naught but a golden glow. To their left the presence of Kilver Forest stretched away before and behind them. The going was increasingly arduous as the land rose; they were traversing the lower slopes of a hill, its summit, faintly visible through the falling snow, was crowned with firs that already wore a thick mantle of white hats. Mr Pixum estimated they had covered a mere league and a half; the major section of their route would be travelled in darkness. He hoped the landmarks he had memorised would remain visible. He gripped the brim of his top hat to prevent it being blown away on the strengthening gusts and strode on.

They were now in the midst of a blizzard. The uphill plod was wearying and when they breasted the slope the wind hit them with renewed force.

'We can't continue in this storm,' shouted The Teapot Man, the upturned teapot on his head was encrusted with snow and being the most diminutive member of the trio, placing one foot in front of the other became more difficult as the snow deepened.

'At least we're now on a downhill slope,' said Mr Fox, turning to his friends, his words barely audible as they were torn away by the wind. In turning, he lost his footing and fell. As he regained his feet, something caught his eye.

'Look! Over there by the edge of the trees, they look like figures. Hard to make them out against the dark firs . . .' Mr Fox frowned. 'The way they moved. Furtive somehow. My hackles are up.' He chuckled. 'The Forest is probably full of Kilvers, whatever they may be.'

'Your wit is only exceeded by your sure-footedness,' said The Teapot Man and immediately fell sprawling in the snow.

The next hour's struggle made it clear to all three that further progress was impossible, they must find shelter before weariness overcame them.

Exhaustion was indeed setting in, their route forced them into the teeth of the blizzard. They discussed entering the Forest and constructing a makeshift shelter but Mr Fox was adamant the dark figures had been keeping pace with them from just inside the tree line. Presently they rounded an outcropping of firs. At the far end of a semi-circular clearing on the slope stood a cabin. A light glowed in the window.

'This is fortunate,' said Mr Pixum, 'and timely.'

'Almost too good to be true,' said Mr Fox.

Gazing at the snow, Mr Pixum felt a curious compulsion to follow it to the ground. Hypnotised, his knees bending, he descended with the falling flakes.

'If it's true it can't be too good.' Mr Pixum climbed to his feet and turned his steps toward the welcoming light. Before they could hammer upon the door it was flung open by a fellow of generous proportions, a great beard, a bald head that gleamed in the lamplight.

'Come in, gentlemen! Come and thaw yourselves out!' He beckoned them inside with a hand that was meaty as a leg of pork; snowflakes fluttered across the threshold, instantly turning into puddles on the floorboards. He heaved the door closed against the wind.

The first thing Mr Pixum noticed was the warmth, it hit him like a feather pillow. The second thing he noticed was how neat the place was. There was a huge wooden table with chairs, four of them, in the centre of the room and affixed to the walls were numerous shelves groaning with rows of bottles, jars and boxes. From the roof timbers hung bunches of dried herbs and on top of an iron oven a cauldron bubbled away; this was, he thought, the source of the aroma, a sublime mix of everything he could think of that appealed to his palate above and beyond his basic need for sustenance.

'I'm Hambardell,' the man said, slamming earthenware bowls on the table, 'Come, sit down, weary travellers and take refreshment.' He brought crusty loaves from the oven and placed one by each of the bowls. 'There'll be time enough for the niceties after you've supped, like.'

As they emptied their bowls of stew and mopped them clean with the last chunks of bread, Hambardell beamed at them. He snatched a bottle and four mugs from a shelf.

'You're very lucky to have made it this far. There's a monster stalking the forest tonight. A young lass from the village is missing, there's a party out searching.'

He flourished the bottle at them. 'This'll warm your bones. My homemade apple brandy, I make it out back.' He took a gulp to set an example. 'Now tell me who you are and what you three seemingly sensible fellows are doing out here in this blizzard.'

His lips were wet as he smiled.

Mr Pixum told Hambardell about their journey to Groque Cat Hall and their thwarted plan to hire a coach or a cart. He didn't think it relevant or wise to mention that the three of them were known as the Feathers of Fate, chosen to maintain equilibrium across the univi by ensuring the Arrow of Destiny was kept upon its true course—nor what this, in practical terms entailed; he merely said they were old friends of Humphrey Harper and left it at that.

Hambardell informed them he lived alone in the cabin, keeping himself busy growing things and making preserves and herbal remedies. He said, 'I'm full o' bright ideas, me, and I put 'em to good use.'

Introductions over, Mr Pixum had to ask what he knew to be the pertinent question.

'Mr Hambardell . . .' he began.

'Just Hambardell, Mr Pixum, that's always been enough for me.'

'As you wish. So tell me, Hambardell, what exactly is this monster you mentioned?'

'A very good question, sir.' He pulled out a chair and sat. 'Aye, very good. Truth is I would've been looking for the girl meself but I saw you coming and knew you'd need looking after. And, I'm ashamed to say, I didn't fancy roaming about in the Forest on a night when the hobs are prowling. The monster, you see, is the worst of the hobs. She's called Lox Gaggymyse the Hobnail, a type of Thurse or Trair. Not anybody you'd've heard of, not being locals, like.'

'That's preposterous,' said The Teapot Man, 'How can such a creature—'

'What perhaps you don't realise,' interrupted Hambardell, 'is that folk are thin on the ground hereabouts and the Forest is nigh on endless, or as good as. The good people stay indoors of a night, stick together, like. They keep their noses out o'things they know nothing about.'

Saw us coming? thought Mr Pixum. 'An unfortunate state of affairs,' he said, 'Can you describe this Lox Gaggymyse to us?'

'Not so unfortunate if they keep out of harm's way, my friend,' he said, leaning forward, this act of shifting his bulk causing his chair to creak. 'She's known locally as the Gaggy or just Gaggy. How to describe her? Well, she's not exactly easy on the eye, great beak of a nose, bulging eyes,' He was enjoying himself, 'A blue face, wild matted hair, yellow pointed teeth and worst of all, her main feature you might say, great spiky talons, claw-like, instead o'hands.' He looked up and sighed, a twinkle in his eyes. 'She eats flesh and soul, one for her own flesh and t'other for her own soul, that's why she's on the prowl.' He stood abruptly. 'Let me show you around.' He ambled through a door in the back of the room which opened into a small passage.

The three friends followed. Hambardell stooped and pulled open a trapdoor revealing a flight of stone steps. 'Careful on the steps, they're uneven.'

As they descended the steps the view gradually revealed itself. It was amazing.

Here was a huge cavern that contained a world of its own. There was an orchard, greenhouses full of fruit and vegetables, there were squashes of all colours and shapes laid out in neat piles on pallets of wood next to bunches of bananas, boxes of apples, potatoes, carrots, parsnips and onions. Beyond the orchard Mr Pixum saw thatched roofs and chimneys. There was a stone barn-like building close to the foot of the steps. 'That's my brewhouse' said Hambardell. The three visitors were awed.

There was a whole village down here, though they could see no inhabitants.

Hambardell watched them, eager for their reactions.

'Staggering,' said Mr Pixum.

'I'm lost for words,' said The Teapot Man.

'*Moi aussi*,' said Mr Fox, sniffing the air.

'What is the source of light?' asked Mr Pixum, his voice a whisper.

Hambardell bounced on his heels and clapped his fleshy palms. 'Bright ideas, Mr Pixum! Didn't I tell you I have bright ideas?'

'And . . . and the heat?'

'More bright ideas.' Hambardell quivered with pleasure. 'Come along, I'll show you more.'

He led the way past the brewhouse, through greenhouses humid and pungent with loam and vegetable exudations, along the village street with its own inn and smithy to a brace of round haystacks between which they could see fields and trees stretching into the distance, those fields nearby bristling with stubble, obviously recently harvested. Eventually they strolled back the way they had come and Hambardell stopped by the brewhouse. 'What do you think?' Hambardell directed their gaze with a wave of his hand.

Before them were three life-sized figures of themselves made entirely from an assortment of fruits and vegetables. The likenesses couldn't be faulted, every detail was there. It was eerie to see themselves fashioned from pumpkins, squashes, carrots, shallots, sheaves of wheat, even potatoes. The curcurbits, umbelliferae, alliums and musas were stitched together with twigs. Hambardell smiled, his lips wet and fleshy.

'I made these in your honour—my distinguished guests.'

Mr Pixum and The Teapot Man walked around the figures, inspecting them, commenting on the craftsmanship. Mr Fox wandered away towards a tree. He touched its bark and felt a slight jolt through his gloves. He touched it again and was rewarded with another jolt. *Too good to be true*: the thought had been running through his mind ever since he had set foot on the cavern floor. He rejoined The Teapot Man. Mr Pixum was nowhere to be seen. Hambardell was busying himself tidying a pile of marrows. The Teapot Man whispered 'Something's not right, I can't sense any kind of source for this power, the heat and light. Have you noticed a bad smell? A rotting smell?'

Another jolt ran through Mr Fox, this time it was purely nervous. 'Why, yes I have, only now am I aware of it, made so by your comment.' He frowned at Hambardell's back, wide as a barn. 'Where's Podmore?'

Mr Pixum rounded the corner of a greenhouse and strode up to them. 'We must leave, this instant!' he said in a low voice, 'My Eye has begun to flicker, we have been deceived!'

Mr Pixum's Magick Eye rarely worked these days and when it did it was but a shadow of what it once was. It had been a gift, a replacement for his lost eye.

'She has a habit of suddenly appearing at your shoulder, like, from nowhere, and when she's that close, well, you know it's too late.' Mr Pixum felt a damp exhalation on the back of his neck and turning he saw it was Hambardell. He was no longer smiling. He grabbed Mr Pixum by his shoulders and threw him to the ground as if he were nothing but a sheaf of wheat. 'I heard you whispering behind my back. Behaviour unbecoming of guests,' he said, licking his lips, 'And you didn't ask the question.' His breathing came in fast thick pants.

'What question?' asked Mr Pixum. He saw Hambardell's great body begin to shimmer.

'The *question* of how the Gaggy deals with her victims.'

'W-what does she do?' Mr Pixum had no desire to know the answer.

Hambardell's nose, had it become a beak? His hands, surely not: great talons curving, clicking together.

'She *enchaunts*!' said Hambardell, rearing above Mr Pixum.

Things happened so fast. Mr Fox threw himself at Hambardell's back and was instantly flung away to land on his own back. Mr Fox didn't see it happen but at the same time as the fox flung himself forward, The Teapot Man plucked the teapotted head from his vegetable likeness, leapt on to a wooden crate and smashed it down on Hambardell's head. He had a fleeting glimpse of "his" head as it transformed into a decaying human head before everything went black.

Mr Fox awoke feeling pain in every sinew. He stretched a little to test for damage before opening his eyes. Nothing serious, although that was possibly due to the numbing cold aching into his bones. Blackness slowly became shades of grey as his eyes became accustomed. A weak luminescence from the window showed him he was in the cabin, though it was no longer a haven of warmth and hospitality, it was derelict. Beside him he heard Mr

Pixum and The Teapot Man stirring.

'Where—? Oh, I see,' said Mr Pixum, levering himself up on to one elbow.

'Great Pan! What has happened to us?'

Not the Great God Pan but The Teapot Man spoke in answer. 'We've been enchaunted. The warm cabin, the stew and bread, the cavern with its glasshouses and fields, all an illusion.'

'This reminds me of The Bright Eyes of the Caraway Seed case,' said Mr Fox.

'How so?' asked The Teapot Man.

'Because it couldn't be more different,' said Mr Fox with a wink.

'Oh not again,' said Mr Pixum, 'This is reminiscent of the Case of the Helm of Gagnir.'

'We fell for the same old trick,' said Mr Fox, 'How tedious.'

'Oh my spine,' Mr Pixum arose wincing. He stretched, massaging his lower back. 'My mind feels defiled by that creature's intrusion. It's illusion is our confusion.'

'So it is.' Mr Fox raised a sardonic brow. 'I would not have guessed.'

The Teapot Man lit a lamp and by its light they saw the squalid, icy cabin.

Mr Fox was about to comment but raised a finger to his lips; voices could be heard outside. The Teapot Man peered out of the window. 'A company of people approaches. I can't make out who they are.'

A man's voice called 'Anyone alive?' and as an afterthought it said 'It's me, Nick, Nick Flackman o't'Gogwhistle.'

'Villagers' said Mr Fox, 'The search party for the missing girl. They must have followed our tracks in the snow.' He opened the door and they stepped outside. The wind had dropped and only a few snowflakes made their lazy way earthwards.

Tracks? *In a blizzard?*

The villagers from Ristholme, carrying lanterns, crowded around the three friends, all seemed relieved to find Mr Pixum and his friends alive and reasonably well. Flackman the landlord was easy to recognise with his head bald as a cabbage nestling in its thicket of black sideburns. There were others they recognised, Simpson the baker, young Dearden the smith, Gash the shepherd and old Frogsiteer the travelling player. They had enjoyed the company of these men last night at the inn, a most convivial evening. There was also a woman present. 'This is Elly Clarence, Madge's ma. I don't suppose you've seen . . . No, of course you haven't' said Flackman, 'You look as if you've been through t'mill.'

'We were tricked by Hambardell who wasn't really Hambardell' said Mr Fox.

'Elijah?' Mrs Clarence spoke to Flackman, her face crimped with anxiety, 'Gaggy walks this night. What chance for Madge?'

'Best not draw any conclusions, Elly,' said Flackman, 'Not while there's still hope.'

Mr Pixum told him all that had happened since they arrived at the cabin.

'An enchauntment' said Flackman, 'the warmth, the vittles, the cavern, all of it.'

He indicated behind them with a nod, 'Even the cabin was an illusion.'

The three Feathers of Fate turned to see no cabin, nothing but the impressions of their three bodies in the snow.

Mr Pixum spoke up. 'Thank you for coming to our aid, Mr Flackman. As you can see, we're a little shaken but otherwise well enough.' He shook himself. 'Time is passing, we really must be on our way now the snow has abated.'

The next instant a starburst of fire hit Frogsiteer the travelling player, engulfing his head in flames. His screech was hideous. Before anyone could react, more balls of fire shot from somewhere to Mr Pixum's left, hitting the villagers at random.

Mr Pixum was pushing Mr Fox and The Teapot Man away from the burning villagers when a familiar voice called out. 'This way, quick, like! It's me, Hambardell!'

The Feathers of Fate had no idea which way to turn but

continued to back away in horror from the stricken party and Hambardell.

'Don't worry, it's all an enchauntment, an illusion, The Gaggy tied me to a tree and left me for dead hours ago. I worked meself free. I heard everything. The fireballs're just one of me bright ideas. Good eh? Come into my cabin, we can keep her out!'

'It didn't keep her out last time,' said Mr Fox.

'You haven't been in there yet,' said Hambardell, 'That was a trick.'

Turning, they saw the cabin once more standing in the clearing, its roof heavy with snow, lamplight glowing enticingly in the window.

The villagers, now charred and smoking, were approaching silently.

There was nothing else for it but to follow Hambardell into the cabin.

With the door barred, Mr Pixum said, 'What is going on here?'

Hambardell said, 'The Gaggy is behind it all, she's a horrible old witch, she is. Them folk out there? They're more of her illusions. She's taken a girl from Ristholme but I rescued her and hid her, then I let Gaggy catch me, I ran back towards the cabin to fool her, like. Gaggy don't know about my trapdoor.'

He stared at them, his face red and moist. 'What did you see?'

'A great cavern lit by bright ideas' said Mr Fox, 'with a whole village and fields, acres of them.'

'She has a vivid imagination, I'll give her that. Come along, I'll show you what it's really like.'

They entered the cabin, it was warm and tidy, just as it had been when they were first welcomed inside. Hambardell lifted the trapdoor and ushered them down the steps into a normal cellar with all its musty aromas, barrels, sacks of potatoes and trays of apples.

Such a shame, thought The Teapot Man, What I could do with those bright ideas . . .

Hambardell shifted a barrel to reveal a girl cowering and

shivering.

Taking up an old sack, Mr Pixum wrapped it around her. He picked her up gently.

'Let's get her upstairs by the stove, Hambardell,' he said.

Meanwhile, Mr Fox scanned the cellar. In the dimmest corner, behind a stack of seed trays, he noticed a low door. He moved the trays aside. The door was crudely fashioned and creaked when he pulled it open. He sensed a stillness behind him. Peering through the doorway he saw a great cavern below him, lit by bright ideas, greenhouses, a village and open fields.

'Somehow it was more impressive the first time around,' said Mr Fox, 'Seems a bit old hat now, Hambardell.'

Hambardell laughed a strange croaking laugh.

He's cackling, thought Mr Fox.

Rage surged through Mr Pixum. He had been fooled one time too many. Time to put an end to Gaggy's farcical game. As he lowered the girl to the floor he spotted a smith's hammer rusted and grey with cobwebs behind a sack of potatoes.

He confronted the maybe-man, maybe something else, with his customary verbosity.

'Hambardell, if that is who you are, prove you are he!'

Hambardell assumed an odd expression, it featured neither triumph nor defeat, though Mr Pixum discerned what may possibly have been a pinch of resignation but if it was, it was the most deadly resignation he'd ever encountered and, to Mr Pixum's Magick Eye, his face flickered with shades of blue.

Mr Fox seized the girl and dashed up the steps, his muscles screaming in pain.

The Teapot Man hesitated, unsure whether to assist Mr Pixum. However, when the Mage of Westrum Powers brought down the hammer on Hambardell's head, he followed swiftly in the Fox's wake, thinking, When it comes to craniums, a lump of illusory old iron beats delusory vegetables every time . . .

Outside in the snow once more, breathless and disorientated, they huddled together for warmth.

'What is your name?' The Teapot Man asked the girl.

'Yonna,' she replied.

'I think the girl we're looking for goes by the name of Madge,' said Mr Pixum.

The girl pouted. 'I'm Yonna. I hate Madge. Elijah—Nick, calls me Yonna.'

'Your mother is evidently fond of the name,' said Mr Pixum.

'That's why I ran away. Tell her to call me Yonna. If she doesn't I'll run away again and Gaggy will kill me and eat me.'

'I'll try, Madge—Yonna,' said Mr Pixum. He was staring at the empty space where the cabin had stood and had disappeared and reappeared and disappeared again.

Was the sky a shade brighter? Or was it a false dawn? At any rate he could see riders approaching from the east, silhouetted against the pale horizon.

'It's Humphrey,' said Mr Fox, 'with the Ristholme search party.'

Waving a jolly halberd, his voice heard but faintly on the rising wind, Humphrey called out.

'Hulloa Feathers of Fate! Hulloa there!'

'Spare horses too,' observed Mr Fox before he went back to examining the weathered scarlet of his hunting coat for scuffs and smuts.

His eye watering from the cold air, Mr Pixum stared wistfully at the riders.

'If only we could be sure that in this instance things really are what they appear to be . . .'

The Lost Boy

Winter twilight coated the creaking architecture of a particular street in the vicinity of Bloomsbury, nevertheless allowing plenty of room for inky shadows to dwell. A lamplighter was even now approaching the lamp standing outside a bookseller's establishment situated on this street. To the north, a dark threat of cloud edged closer, more than hinting at the possibility of snow before the morrow.

Mr Pixum and Mrs Mavis Enderby, his housekeeper, alighted from a cab and watched as the bookseller's was illuminated wanly by the lamp. The building was situated on the corner of two streets that diverged into the crepuscular distance, giving the place a triangular plan with the shop-door set in the very place where the elevations of both streets' frontages converged. From above it could be said the premises resembled a reasonably-sized slice of cheese. It was a building of three storeys with the addition of a small cupola perched above the radiused corner some thirty feet above the front door. On the ground floor, along both diverging sides of the shop, were large windows consisting of small panes of glass, through which prospective patrons could peruse the various editions on display within.

Above the windows a well-painted fascia board proclaimed this business to be:

RAPHAEL SOAMES, BOOKSELLER.
ANTIQVARIAN, RARE & ARCANE BOOKS

Mr Pixum noticed how well-illuminated was the interior, lamps and candles had been placed frequently about the room; he could clearly see ceiling to floor bookshelves lining the walls and also free-standing shelves, crammed with richly bound tomes. He could make out a figure who must surely be the man who was the cause of his current visitation.

Mr Pixum stood a moment and recalled the reason he and Mrs Enderby had arrived at his door this evening.

Half an hour ago Mr Pixum was, as usual, reclining at his snug fireside with a decidedly fascinating book when the doorbell rang. Mrs Enderby, who was, as usual, busying herself somewhere in Mr Pixum's town house, clumped downstairs to answer it. A minute later she burst breathlessly into Mr Pixum's pleasant doze and handed him a note delivered by messenger.

The contents galvanised Mr P into action.

'Have the messenger wait!' called Mr Pixum. He scribbled out messages and instructed Mrs Enderby to send them off before throwing a few things into his carpetbag. Mrs Enderby, who had read the message over her master's shoulder, wrapped her shawl about her ample shoulders and accompanied him out of the door.

Evidently in a voluble mood, not a rare thing, his housekeeper said, 'Wot a nice fresh evenin'. I 'ope it's like this when I takes me trip, an' not pourin' wi' rain.'

'A trip, Mrs E? Somewhere pleasant I trust?'

'Vauxhall Wossname... Vauxhall *Gardens*, that's the one. Saved up me shillin's. I loves farworks, me.'

'A splendid place to visit! The music, the fireworks, the lamps and all kinds of entertainment. But do take care, won't you? Thieves infest every shadow within the Gardens.'

'Let 'em try thievin' from me! They'll be cryin' for their mamas hif they tries anythin'! Oh I'm lookin' forward to me day awf, I am! Now then, let's go 'an do wot we 'ave to!'

'Please do not trouble yourself, Mrs Enderby,' Mr Pixum urged.

'Hif yer please, sir, but in a sitiwation sech as this, it's likely the lad will need a bit o' motherin."

'I worked for Mr Soames for over twenty years,' said the bookseller, Augustus Eldred, a bespectacled, plump figure wearing a soft felt hat and a velvet jacket of bottle green, replying to Mr Pixum's query, 'and on his deathbed Mr Soames announced he'd bequeathed his business to me, a gift for which I shall be forever grateful.'

He had hardly ended his sentence when the shop-door flew inward with a bang, announcing the arrival of Mr Pixum's friends.

Of late, Mr Fox had been seen sporting a variety of headwear; on this occasion a tricorne hat graced his vulpine pinnacle. His immaculate apparel of red hunting coat, mustard waistcoat and white gloves completed his outfit. He sniffed and reached for his kerchief.

'*Il y a une odeur de moisi dans cette librairie. Je pourrais éternuer!*'

This, hopefully, to spare the unfortunate proprietor.

His companion, The Teapot Man, looked every bit as he always did: green greatcoat, red trousers and the inverted teapot upon his head gleaming lustrously in the lamplight.

Mr Pixum clapped his hands. 'Eldred! Now we're all here you must explain the situation to us—explain in as much detail as you can and leave nothing out! Nothing!'

Eldred proceeded to explain.

'Dabbling, sir! Dabbling! That's the beginning of it all.'

Mr Eldred's son, Franklin, Mr Eldred said, was in grave danger, perhaps mortal danger. The bookseller told how Frankie, as his son was more familiarly known, was something of a bookworm. More than that, he took after his father in that he had a special interest in the magickal arts. From an early age he had pored over great dusty grimoires in the back of the bookshop. Having reached his tenth year his father thought he would come to no harm if he conducted a few small experiments on his own—after all, Eldred senior had done the very same himself at his son's age and lived to tell the tale. Frankie had been up in his playroom on the second floor all day. He used this room as his "hideout" and spent many solitary hours alone in there. Eldred nevertheless began to feel uncomfortable.

'He'd been far too quiet. Something felt wrong.'

Eldred had tramped upstairs to the second floor "hideout" and found the room empty. Notably there was a magick circle painted on the floor. He called out his son's name.

'His voice came from a trunk. I thought he must be trapped inside but all it contained was a pile of old leaves.'

'Dead leaves in the trunk?' asked Mr Fox with incredulity.

'No! Leaves from books!' Eldred resumed his tale: Frankie was heard calling for help, as if from a great distance. There was a notebook open upon the table that enabled Eldred to piece together what the boy had been up to. Frankie, it appeared, had disappeared because he had conjured a very tricky demon "for fun" and failed to control it. The demon, OuaxDaz'imoth, had been far too cunning for the boy and whisked him away to wherever he was now, in some horrible place in a parallel universe.

'This other universe would appear to have various points of nearness, one of which resides in the same place as that which the trunk occupies,' said Mr Pixum.

Eldred, knowing more than a little about magick, had immediately set up an invoking ritual and summoned OuaxDaz'imoth with the aim of forcing the demon to return his boy.

'I made sure the demon kept within the Triangle of Art but even so, he tricked me,' said Eldred, grimacing and breathing in short gasps, 'I forced him to concede but I couldn't push past a certain point; it was all I could do to keep control of the situation. He told me he would leave a key and a keyhole. All I have to do is fit one into the other and Frankie is returned to me. But there's a catch. I have to find them before sunrise tomorrow or they will dematerialise forever.'

He banged his fist on the tabletop. 'The wretched demon would do no more—and I hadn't the power to force him. I suspect he only granted the favour of the key in order to see me suffer the more.' Eldred buried his face in his hands.

'No one can command OuaxDaz'imoth,' grated Mr Pixum, 'One should never invoke him!'

Eldred finished his tale, saying that he had sought the key and keyhole without success, panicked, calmed down and sent for Mr Pixum, knowing of him as a scholar but more significantly for his reputation as a mage.

'Time really is of the essence,' said Mr Pixum, as cool as a dew-comber, 'but before we act I must tell you a little more about alternate universes, or "univi" as I call them.' He cupped his hand above his eye, tilted his head and peered into the distance.

'If you look *askance* in the correct way you can see these worlds from other universes interpenetrating each other yet separate. Look down yonder street,' he gestured towards the window, '*askance* your gaze and see the long tunnels appear with many different worlds floating through in every direction, each one complete but also part of all the others, because, as you know, Creation is One.' Mr Pixum looked around those assembled and actually grinned. 'Flittings, creepings, scurryings, lurkings, comings forth and meltings away into shadows—all can be glimpsed by the correctly *askanced* eye. This is the origin of the phrase "Look at it this way." New horizons beckon, new worlds unfold just out of reach, hidden dangers deliver a delicious thrill, different light illumines strange cities and unknown suns cast shadows long and leery across gazooming alien landscapes.'

'I think we should get down to business.'

This remark from The Teapot Man.

'You are entirely correct. It will be quite simple,' stated Mr Pixum confidently, 'I will easily spot the key with my Magick Eye.' He flipped up his eyepatch and a beam of blue light shot forth only to droop and fade away to nothing.

'What is this?' asked the mystified mage.

Augustus Eldred cleared his throat. 'I believe there is a warding field cast about these premises. I became aware of it when I tried something myself a little while ago. OuaxDaz'imoth's ingenuity at work, I assumed.'

Mr Pixum made an impatient gesture. 'Pah! It's dead. Nothing left in this Eye—it is useless.'

He flipped down his eyepatch.

'What shall we do?' asked Eldred.

'Search!' shouted Mr Pixum, 'Look high and low as you have never looked before! And make haste, time is passing!'

They decided to begin with the second floor.

He awoke with a shock. He had been slammed on to a hard surface.

'Oh horror!'

He was being cut up—literally chopped into horizontal slices. His mind went numb. What had he done to deserve this?

'I don't believe it!' A shudder passed through him from top to tail. He knew this was worse than the worst nightmare he could ever have imagined. Now he was being sliced lengthways! 'Oh horror! Horror!'

Then he remembered: it all made sense. Now he knew what it was all about. He'd been so groggy from his sleep that he'd completely forgotten he was a carrot. A huge sigh escaped him.

'That's alright then.' He was fulfilling his purpose. He was an orange-coloured casserole decoration, a groundsnack, a horsecrunch, a peg with leaves attached; in short, an edible root.

These last thoughts emanated from him as Mavis Enderby, wife of a permanently missing seaman, swept his bits up and dropped them into the pot. Was this good lady aware of the sensibilities of the vegetable she had dispatched with such rough but competent dexterity? Far from it. Mrs Enderby had taken herself off to the kitchen to prepare a hearty soup.

'These fellas will need some fewell in 'em ter keep 'em goin."

Not knowing what it was they were looking for made the search rather confusing. Mr Eldred was instructed to look over everything calmly and remark anything he had not seen before. Mr Fox and The Teapot Man, both very aware of the short time they had, proceeded with great enthusiasm to latch on to anything they could pick up .

'Is this the key?'

'No, it's a spoon.'

'Is this the key?'

'No, that's an inkwell.'

'Is this the key?'

'No, it's a stuffed owl.'

'Is this the key?'

'No and neither is this.'

'Ouch!'

'Is this the key?'

'No, it's by doze!'

'Is this the key?'

'No, it's a calfskin fiddle.'

And so on.

The rocking horse, a toy from Frankie's younger days, emitted a faint but ghastly howl. Everyone stopped their frantic search and stared at it.

'*Ooooaaah! Help me! Help!*'

'That's Frankie's voice!' declared Eldred.

'It would seem that the rocking horse occupies another point where the barrier between Frankie's world and ours is thin,' said Mr Pixum, 'I wonder whether he can hear us?'

'Frankie! Frankie!' called his father, 'Can you hear me?'

'*Father!*' called the rocking horse, the tiny voice coming from a great distance, '*Father! Help Me!*'

'We'll soon have you back!' called Mr Pixum, trying to sound as if he believed what he was saying.

'*Help me! There's something out there in the dark!*'

'What is it?' asked Mr Pixum and Eldred in unison.

'I can't see anything! It's too dark. I can hear it scratching. It draws closer! Help me!'

Mr Pixum considered the hours remaining until daybreak but refrained from stating the obvious.

Later, Mr Fox was rummaging through a box of bits and pieces in the corner of the dining room on the first floor when he heard it again, this time coming from a longcase clock.

'Heeeelp! Father! Help me!'

The fox straightened and raised his eyebrows.

'L'horloge demande de l'aide!' He shook his head and resumed his search.

During his determined inventory of the ground floor, The Teapot Man picked up a smallish tub. He tried to open it, but without success: the top was too tightly fixed. He handed it to Eldred.

'Can you open this tub?'

Eldred was too worried to argue. He took the tub and wrenched at the top. It did not budge. He gave it another great tug and the top suddenly shot across the room in a cloud of white powder.

'French chalk!' exclaimed the bookseller, 'Now we'll never find anything in here!'

'On the contrary,' said Mr Pixum from the doorway, 'Your chalk dust has revealed a previously invisible item after all.'

Indeed, seeming to hang in the air between the racks was a peculiar device made visible by a thin coating of chalk dust: it comprised an equilateral triangle, apex upwards, with small straight rods sprouting from the centre of the outside edge of each side at an angle of ninety degrees, each with a small sphere at its end. Most interesting though, was the perfectly conventional keyhole in the centre of the triangle.

Everyone cheered.

'But what the devil are you doing with French chalk?' asked the Teapot Man.

'I use it to remove grease stains from the pages of books,'

replied Mr Eldred, 'I also dust it between the leaves of books if I am to gild the edges. During the gilding process it prevents the leaves from sticking.'

'Ah, *Craie de Champagne*,' murmured a knowledgeable Mr Fox.

Mr Pixum held up the tub.

'Do you have any more of these?'

'Perhaps. Somewhere in here,' Eldred muttered as he rooted in the back of a work-cupboard.

'Ah ha! Here we are!'

An observer standing in the street, looking through the windows on any floor of the establishment known as 'Raphael Soames, Bookseller' (although the title of proprietor had now passed to one Augustus Eldred) would have been unable not to notice that, despite the golden glow indicative of the presence of lamps and candles, not one single detail could be discerned through the glazing. It was as if all of the air inside the edifice containing the business, which yet bore the appellation of the late Soames, was made opaque with roiling white clouds.

In the kitchen, Mrs Enderby uncovered her pot, blowing chalk-dust from the lid a she did so.

'*Heeelp! I don't want to die! Help!*'

'Talkin' soup! Well I'll be a gotch-gutted glue-pot! Some *fegary*, that is!'

Now residing in London for much of the time Mrs Enderby delighted in the appropriation—and misappropriation—of the local idiom, a favour she had similarly dispensed with regard to the vernacular of her native Norfolk.

Waiting for the dust to settle taxed their nerves. Mr Pixum was forced to remind the company (as if they had not already known) that but two hours remained until dawn. The Teapot Man twitched, drew strange symbols in the air and jigged about with small steps; Mr Fox, in search of famous foxes in history, pored over a volume but gave it less than half of his attention; Mr Eldred scraped his feet back and forth and rubbed his hands together, no one meeting another's eyes. To a man (or a fox) they were as dusty as a pharoah's mummy.

Presently, Mr Pixum announced:

'The chalk has settled enough! Let us resume!'

White faced and grim, they began with the ground floor and steadily worked their way upwards.

With less than an hour to sunrise, four dejected searchers stood in Frankie's "hideout."

'Nothing!' declared Mr Eldred and he began to sob.

'A keyhole with no key. Hmmm . . .' mused The Teapot Man.

'We've looked everywhere. The demon has fooled us.'

'Not necessarily!' Mr Pixum spoke with vigour.

'Eldred! Show us the roof!'

The air was still and cold. It was no longer pitch dark nor yet by any means light; the snow cloud had passed over and left a fine powdering to cover the rooftops for as far as they could see. A scattering of stars twinkled above. On another occasion the three friends would have made time to enjoy the view but there was a good deal of rooftop to explore. There were leaden gulleys, pitched slates, chimneys, gutters.

'The snow will help us,' remarked Mr Fox, his breath steaming in the pre-dawn air, 'As if it were Nature's French chalk, eh?'

They stepped carefully about the rooftop, occasionally slipping, gasping and cursing. Their handprints and footprints were everywhere. Time crept by with ever more haste.

'There! Look!' It was Eldred himself who spotted it and why not? After all it was his roof. All eyes fixed upon the object and then:

'Great Pan!' exclaimed Mr Pixum.

'Oh save us!' Eldred groaned.

In the sky, as if painted on to a huge invisible glass dome, appeared an enormous grey-white, two dimensional image of a creature resembling a wide skeletal monkey, its teeth bared in an idiotic grin, its gaze malevolent. Its fingers were splayed, giant semi-transparent spiders, twitching and each time they twitched, they replicated themselves. The monkey-thing began to swing around the night's dome as if on a swivel, duplicating itself into three wide monkeys, multi-spiderhands and all.

'Stand fast!' shouted Mr Pixum, 'It's only a show of gloating from OuaxDaz'imoth, a stupid wardance or something. He knows he's defeated. There's nothing he can do to stop us now!'

A spiked finial that doubled as a lightning conductor rose from the top of the cupola. Perched precariously on the tip of the spike, outlined by a frosting of snow, was a triangular shaped object, the twin of the keyhole downstairs. The only difference was the keybit with its pattern of ward-cuts protruding from the centre.

'Hoorah!' cried Eldred, 'We can save Frankie!'

A short ladder was fetched from below and Mr Pixum, having volunteered to climb up and retrieve the key, proceeded to do so.

Mr Eldred, The Teapot Man and Mr Fox held the ladder steady. Soon it began to spring a little beneath Mr Pixum's weight.

The lightning conductor also began to spring a little with the weight of the ladder and Mr Pixum but the key remained perched.

Mr Pixum was doing his best to keep his balance as slowly he mounted the rungs. He looked down over the cupola and the parapet and saw the snowy street so far below, which was a mistake as it made his head swim. In spite of this he kept his balance and continued to climb.

His companions stood below, rigidly clamping the ladder, their eyes on the climber and the key, not daring to breathe.

The movement above caught Mr Pixum's eye—the cavortings of OuaxDaz'imoth—his attention wavered, his balance lost for a second, his foot stepped into space. His fingers, numb with cold, slipped from the ladder.

His companions held their breath.

Mr Pixum felt his body falling to one side. He grasped frantically for purchase but gravity was pulling at him. The fingers of his left hand caught hold of a rung. Now he hung from the ladder, his legs swaying above the cobbles far below.

He heard gasps from the rooftop.

Swinging his legs back and forth, he managed to wrap a leg around the ladder and was able to clamp his right hand on to a rung. With a great effort he secured himself and clung there, panting like a thirsty dog.

Moments later he scrambled his feet back on to the rungs but he was too late: the extra vibrations created by his struggle caused the spike to shudder enough to dislodge the key.

Falling, it relinquished its mantle of snow—and disappeared.

After much searching, as if myopic men trying to locate a pair of spectacles, they were forced to admit that the key was no longer anywhere on the roof.

'It must have fallen into the street,' stated The Teapot Man.

There followed a thorough search of the streets surrounding the bookseller's shop. Time fairly galloped along as dawn approached. At one point they found themselves reading theatre bills on the wall, and looked at each other resignedly, admitting they were stumped.

After a long time, time they could not afford to waste and yet time they could no longer think of any adequate use for, they repaired into the shop, from whence they were called into the kitchen by Mrs Enderby.

''Ave yerselves somethin' warm,' she said, 'I've made yer a thick soup ter keep yer sperits up! Yer can't keep on going without some goodniss inside yer! You four look a right passel o' snowmen if hever I saw one!'

Mrs Enderby began to ladle a steaming broth into four earthenware dishes.

Eldred pushed his dish to one side and turned away.

Mr Fox, when all else failed, fell back on his vanity. He'd caught a glimpse of himself as he passed a mirror and was mortified. He wasn't in the least concerned how the others looked—it was his own appearance that worried him. He began to dust his sleeves and shoulders, clouds of chalk-dust erupting from his gloves. Admitting to himself that there was little more he could do for his coat, with a flourish he removed his three corner hat, intending to beat the dust from it. Coincident with this action was a clunk and a splash.

'*Watchwhatyerdoin'!*' squawked Mrs Enderby, staring at the stained table cloth.

Mr Pixum stared at the soup . . .

The clock struck the quarter. The street, decidedly lighter, was quiet.

Mr Pixum grabbed what appeared to be a handful of soup and dashed from the kitchen.

And now, as usual, we move time forward by an hour or even two. Our friends, together with Mr Eldred and his son, Franklin, are relaxing by a merry coal fire in the parlour behind the bookshop.

The relieved father has boxed his son's ears for causing such to-do. Soup and toast have been gratefully consumed and the kettle whistles happily on the hob, ready for another pot of tea.

That tea. That all-important cup of tea. That *teapot infusion pouring from the spout* experience. The aroma and the drinking of it, the assimilation of the brew, letting the realisation of it permeate mind and spirit and body, putting the day's events into their proper place, thus closing the episode of the lost boy with health, humour and heart.

Invigorating, life-affirming, refreshing tea worked its own magick. The light in the eyes glittering in the sockets in the skull of The Teapot Man, alive with his peculiar, particular knowledge of this ontological vignette, with the perspicacity of his knowing, the root of which resides deep in his blood, his cells, his history, his past *and* his future—comes forth, upwelling from that root's depths, and, like a theatre poster pasted across his face, it can be as easily read and as clearly understood. With rolling eyes and never-faltering grin, it says:

'Whatever is and is not, whatever has been and will be, whatever shifts and whatever remains unmoved in the Webs of Fate, we have done what we *could* do and that *right action* is a pragmatic virtue in itself. Our hearts and minds were, for the most part, on track—which fact alone drew the Webs to where we wanted them, for, situated outside of time, there is no past and no future to consider: the present, in that place, is always all, paradoxical though it may seem.'

Although The Teapot Man has conveyed much from a mere facial expression, there are few that can read *quite* so much from it. To Mr Pixum and Mr Fox it is plainer than the poster pasted on the brickwork of the bookseller's proclaiming the opening of Mr Samuel Foote's comic lectures at the Haymarket Theatre. Their ease of perception, of course, is largely due to the fact that they are connected as friends—*and Feathers of Fate . . .*

The boy, chief culprit and rescued victim of this little drama, sits in his little chair, lovingly crafted for him by his father, his nose buried in a book. He looks for all the world like a boy who has recently enjoyed a game of snowballs with his chums and, having worn the novelty out of this seasonal sport, returned to the family hearth, the better to thaw out his fingers.

Desultory conversation ebbs and flows. Mrs Enderby has begun a little light snoring, exhausted, poor dear, by the night's excitement.

The discussion touches upon many subjects: books, demons, books, dabblers, books again, until Mr Pixum sighs and stretches his arms.

'I think it is time we took ourselves home,' he says.

Mr Eldred, happy and emotional, weeps his thanks once again.

The Teapot Man prods Mrs Enderby into a spluttering semblance of being awake. The little company prepares to disperse

into this bright and frosty morn.
    'Where's Frankie?' cries Mr Eldred.
    Without a word, four pairs of feet clatter up the staircase.

The Box

Mr Fox was on his way to visit Mr Pixum. He passed by an archway through which he glimpsed market stalls. He drew to a halt to give himself time to think: would he carry on immediately to Pixum's or would he browse the market?

It was late afternoon, the sky was lowering and the traders were beginning to pack away their wares. The fox threaded his way through the stalls, dodging surly stall holders and attempting to avoid stepping in anything untoward. The market was held in a courtyard walled-in by the backs of ancient buildings and the ivy-covered walls of closes and gardens. The low winter sunshine lit up ridges of striped canvas awnings above the stalls on the far side and deceptively invested the irregular rooftops and chimneys on the skyline with a warm rubescent glow.

In a corner, where two ancient walls met beneath a twisted, moss-covered tree that grew out of a crack riven in the stones, a string of coloured lanterns caught his eye. Had they not been lit, Mr Fox would have passed by the dismal corner unaware that it contained anything but shadows. As he made his way towards them, the better to see what they represented, a market boy tugged his sleeve.

'If you was thinkin' o' visitin' old Fadder Regoat's stall, I recommend you thinkin' again, pardonin' my for'ard manners.'

'Why on earth not?' asked Mr Fox, 'Is he in competition with your mater's stall? That's a low trick, young knave, and it makes me all the more determined to give the old fellow my custom. Get along with you!'

'On yer own 'ead, then,' said the boy, hurrying off, 'It seems doin' a feller a good turn ain't appreciated 'round 'ere.'

A cloud-bank had risen swiftly up the sky, spreading rapidly from east to west, blindfolding the sun. Thus bedimmed, the marketplace transformed itself into a chiaroscuro of dreamlike shapes.

As he neared the stall, the fox saw it was piled with an untidy assortment of items, some of which, even as he watched, were disappearing into open packing cases placed close by. More such cases had been loaded on to a cart that stood behind the stall. A broad but short figure, wearing a hat with an extremely wide and floppy brim, was obviously closing down his business for the day.

'Mind if I have a quick look before you pack away your wares?' asked the fox.

The man, presumably Fadder Regoat himself, raised his head, allowing Mr Fox to discern, beneath the hat's brim, nothing but a bulbous nose; the rest of the face remained in shadow.

The voice was abrupt and phlegmy. 'Give you a minute, no longer. Unless you're buying.'

Looking so enticing in the pool of oily gold cast by the nearest lamp, the box captured Mr Fox's attention straightaway. With its intricate carving just discernible through a layer of grime, it exuded something . . . unusual.

'That would clean up rather well,' mused Mr Fox to himself, 'I can see it sitting upon my desk, polished to a lustre. Certainly a conversation piece.' He was about to begin haggling the price down but it seemed the practiced eye of the market trader had pre-empted him.

'A crown, take it or leave it.'

Mr Fox was wary, 'That's a suspiciously fitting sum for such a piece. It *is* genuine? Not merely card and plaster?'

'It's all natural,' confirmed Regoat, 'and all the relief work is the real thing. It's the authentic, certainly.' The man's breathing sounded like bubbles rising through mud.

Glancing about, the fox was surprised to see that the market area was now deserted. How did everyone manage to pack up and scuttle off so quickly? He supposed that, as the light had faded and the cold was biting harder, the other browsers and erstwhile stallholders were eager to get home to a warm fire, as was he eager to put himself before the glow of Pixum's hearth.

'Good. I'll take it.'

'You'll have to take what's inside, too.'

'I only want the box. You're welcome to keep the contents.'

'It's the condition of sale,' said the old man, 'Take the lot or leave it. It's all the same to me.'

Mr Fox was annoyed. 'Why do I have to take something I don't want? What's inside it anyway?'

'You don't have to take anything. I told you it's—'

'Yes, I know, it's all the same to you. A strange sort of market trader you are.'

'It's a book. Just an old book and something. Make your mind up, I'm not for waiting about.'

'Very well, I'll take the blasted book and all.' Mr Fox fished in his pocket and handed over a crown.

Regoat dropped the coin into a small purse and, using a short piece of candle, pushed the box over to Mr Fox's side of the board.

Mr Fox picked up the box—it was surprisingly heavy—and stalked away. He wasn't sure, but he thought he may have heard a chuckle, a very phlegmy chuckle, follow him through the archway.

The Teapot Man arrived early and stood before the fire to restore the circulation in his hands and feet: they had been thoroughly nipped on his journey through the winter streets.

It was to be merely an evening of pleasant companionship; the Feathers of Fate would while away their time in pleasant conversation by the fireside, something that happened too infrequently of late, all three had been busy with the inevitable calls upon their time made by their separate lives.

Tonight would give them an opportunity to bring one another up to date with their goings-on, fuelled by good wine from Mr Pixum's cellar and just enough of a repast from Mrs Enderby's kitchen to satisfy their stomachs.

Pending the arrival of Mr Fox, Mr Pixum and The Teapot Man peered through the panes, watching the clouds unburden themselves at last, having waited until it was almost dark to do this, and now delighting in dropping countless flurries of flakes as large as quail eggs into the empty air above the city, where they swirled and spiraled as they floated earthwards.

After snow had been falling for only half an hour, the view from Mr Pixum's window was transformed. Rooftops, teapots, window sills and pavements were thick with sugar icing. Where light spilled from windows, aprons of gold stretched across pavements and changed the dancing flakes into fireflies. The coming night quickly turned the white blanket into ever-deepening shades of blue.

The doorbell rang.

Mr Pixum and The Teapot Man glanced at each other. They heard Mrs Enderby calling, 'Alright! 'Old yer 'orses!' And then the sound of the street door opening and then slammed to a moment later. A stamping on the doormat. A rattle as a cane was dropped into the hallstand. A thud. Footsteps creaking up the stairs.

Mr Fox burst into the room, brushing snowflakes from his shoulders and whiskers. Mr Pixum saw the fox was shivering, so without asking, he poured his friend a glass of mulled wine from one of several bottles that stood warming in the fireplace, topping-up The Teapot Man's glass and his own at the same time.

'Good afternoon, dear friends,' said Mr Fox, raising his glass. 'Your health!'

An hour or so later, two of the three friends lounged—relaxed and warmed by both fire and wine—having exchanged enough tidbits from their recent doings to consider themselves as up to date as they cared to be. Mr Fox sat, one knee thrown across the other, his boot tapping the air in time to some inner tune, a tune that appeared to be speeding up if the rhythm of his toe was any indication. He drummed his fingers on the arm of his chair.

'You seem a little tense, Bertie,' ventured Mr Pixum.

'No . . . I don't think so,' replied the fox vaguely, his eyes darting about the room.

Mr Pixum also looked around the room, saw nothing unusual and allowed himself to take pleasure in the firelight playing on the gilded frame of an ancestral portrait.

'He looks as if there's something on his mind,' said The Teapot Man.

'There's nothing on my mind!' said the fox, in the manner of someone with something on his mind.

Mr Pixum's and The Teapot Man's gazes combined and rested gently, coaxingly, upon Mr Fox. The mantel clock ticked away. The fire settled with a crack and a rustle.

The mantel clock ticked on . . .

'Oh, all right!' snapped the fox, 'I was thinking about how familiar things cease to mean anything, whereas unfamiliar things contain meaning as if it were stored energy.'

'Everything means something,' said Mr Pixum, 'and there is a choice here: either you wait, ponder and allow the meaning to deliver itself up—or you invest it with the meaning you wish it to have. It's your decision.'

'What about the *truth* of it?' asked the fox, 'Surely the second option allows a surfeit of choice? For instance, two weeks last Wednesday, when a roof-tile fell as I passed beneath, narrowly missing me, I could assign to it the meaning that it's a sign that my Aunt Belinda would descend upon me a week last Friday, when she inevitably told off her list of my faults as usual, in return for which, she expected me to provide her with a sumptuous tea, my eternal gratitude and a cart-load of compliments. To assign the first event to the second event is absurd. I merely connected them at random, knowing full well there was no such connection. The falling tile and the descending aunt are two separate accidents.'

'So it would seem,' said Mr Pixum, 'although your conclusion is somewhat hasty. The Teapot Man may have something to say about *meaning*. However, what I was getting at was not quite so abstruse. My coat, for example, already means something to me, several things, in fact. First, it is a coat, therefore it means precisely what any coat means in all its coatfulness: keeps out the cold, useful pockets et cetera—but also, it has personal meaning. For instance, I chose this coat by conveying to my tailor exactly what I wanted it to be, the style, the cut, the cloth, the lining, the buttons. The result is that it means more than "coat" in the abstract; it is the coat I chose in particular, to suit my personal taste. Secondly, when I wear it, see it, touch it, go forth in it, it evokes all the experiences we have had together, imbuing it not only with the cold status of mnemonic but that of close companion with which I have shared a large part of my life. There is a massive web of interconnections concerning this coat and my life—fate links us together in so many ways. To summarise: the meaning of this coat is in its value to me, which is not inconsiderable.'

'If I understand your *meaning* correctly, you have just explained that your coat means a lot to you.' Mr Fox rose to his feet and refilled his glass. Mr Pixum offered up his glass but the fox merely handed him the bottle and resumed his seat. 'Brevity, Podmore, has never been one of your virtues.'

Mr Pixum poured for The Teapot Man and himself, making quite a point of it.

'As you well know,' said The Teapot Man, 'my meaning is all about the interconnectedness of things. My purpose is to try to recognise particular connections and interpret them. It is not an exact science due to a multitude of subtleties and the small matter of infinite possibilities, but I can assure you that all of existence, and all the systems within it, have meaning, whether they are familiar or not. We are each of us processes comprised of a series of events. We have meaning both as a whole entity and also right down to each particle of energy of which we are comprised.'

'Entities? Energies? What have they to do with anything?' Mr Fox left his chair and stood in front of the fire, careful to keep his brush away from the flames. 'What I want to know—what I asked—is why do some unfamiliar things have so much meaning? Why do they have such power? I may pass by a palace a thousand times and not even notice it after the first two or three but should I visit an out of the way place and experience that which I have never before set eyes upon, for instance, the sight of the merest wooded slope at twilight, a huddle of snow-covered cottages, an overgrown ruin or a group of menhirs lashed by a storm, my senses are quickened with the power of its meaning.'

Mr Pixum smiled. 'The power is unfamiliarity,' he said, 'New things, strange things, unexpected things, a break with the accustomed, have the power—the power of novelty—to awaken your sense of meaning. A strange cottage, humble or no, has no more intrinsic meaning than your own familiar hearth!'

Here The Teapot Man interjected mysteriously, 'Unless, of course, it has.'

Ignoring this remark, Mr Pixum continued, 'And yet, though you may love your hearth, its very familiarity causes you to take it for granted.'

Mr Fox gave a dismissive bat of his hand. 'I know all that. Bah! I also know what you meant about connections. Interconnectedness. You can glue the messenger-boy to everything but what if the acid web eats it? *Dieux de la vérité*! I was waiting for you to get to the point. I really don't need your condescension. When I consider connections, I rarely get too far beneath the surface of things. To me it feels just like clutching at so many straws. *Obscuris vera involvens*. Too much poking about behind the scenes is debilitating to me. While it's true I make the occasional leap and find a link between certain events, I prefer to leave that sort of thing to others, if you understand what I mean?'

'Oh, I understand *your* meaning,' said The Teapot Man, 'That takes the minimum of effort.' In response to the flash in Mr Fox's yellow eyes, he quickly added, 'And I understand the value of your meaning cannot be underestimated.'

Disconcertingly, the fox grinned. 'I came across something this afternoon that seems to me to be full of intrigue. Full of *meaning*. Perhaps it will have the same effect upon the two of you?'

'But how can—?' began Mr Pixum.

'I'll go and fetch it,' said Mr Fox, 'It's in the hall.' He dashed from the room, and, as he descended the staircase, he silently congratulated himself on his steering the conversation to *just the right place* . . .

Mr Pixum could see The Teapot Man was as mystified as he was. Was the fox playing some sort of prank? There was no doubt Mr Fox had stage-managed the previous conversation for his own ends, but what were those ends? Nothing for it but to await developments. Wait! There was something he could do to ensure Mr Fox would not get things all his own way. He rang for Mrs Enderby to bring up the supper. Perhaps he was being a spoil-sport but the thought of being thus manipulated had rankled.

Mr Fox struggled into the room with his burden, closely followed by Mrs Enderby carrying a tray covered with a white cloth.

'I presume you have no objection to taking a light repast at this point?' asked Mr Pixum, knowing his friend's fondness for victuals at any time of the day.

Mr Fox, despite being annoyed, was no match for his own appetite.

'Um, none at all. In fact it may be advantageous to take some nourishment before we proceed further.' He placed the box in the centre of the hearthrug and was first to help himself to a plate of pasties, cheeses and pickles.

Half an hour later, the three friends gathered around the strange-looking box.

'What does it contain?' asked The Teapot Man.

'I have had no opportunity to open it yet,' said Mr Fox.

'These relief carvings are unusual,' said Mr Pixum, 'and yet there is something familiar about them that I can't place.'

'Do you see,' said the fox, 'how it seems to vibrate with "meaning"?'

'It vibrates with something, certainly,' said Mr Pixum, 'It exudes a baneful peccancy yet there is a strange elegance to its repulsive symmetry. Is that why you were drawn to it?'

'I—I can't quite explain it,' said Mr Fox, 'I was on my way here when I passed the market. The next thing I knew I was making a beeline for a stall tucked away in the far corner beneath a wall. Ah . . . there were coloured lamps strung about it . . . I was rude to a boy; he tried to dissuade me from visiting the stall. This box commanded my attention . . .'

'Hmm . . . Curious. It would seem the stallholder aroused disquiet among the other market traders. I think it's time we looked inside.' Mr Pixum knelt beside the box and ran his fingers over the ridges and curlicues carved in relief on its surface. He ran a finger along the edge.

'Here's the catch, see?'

With his thumbnail, he slid a brass button to one side. There was a click and the lid lifted a fraction. Mr Pixum opened it fully to reveal a book and a glass vial nestled snugly in the indentations of what looked like a padded lining of soft goatskin. An aroma was released: it was astringent, chemical, slightly unpleasant. He lifted out the book.

'Great Pan! This weighs more than any box of this size I have ever encountered!'

The Teapot Man picked up the vial. 'This is unnaturally heavy, too,' he said. It contained a powder the colour of earth. Perhaps it was?

Mr Fox looked on, pleased to have supplied such a novel item.

The book was bound in hide wrinkled and darkened with age and on it's cover was pasted a label that read: "*The Book of Humphrey Stipkins*".

Mr Pixum took his seat by the fire and opened the book. He read in silence for a few minutes.

'This is a journal, handwritten. There are no dates I can see as yet. It smells of age, though. The pages are very thick, a heavy vellum, possibly.'

As Mr Pixum read on, Mr Fox poured more mulled wine for all three of them. The Teapot Man and Mr Fox went over to the window and gazed out. Several inches of snow had landed and more continued to fall.

Eventually, Mr Pixum interrupted his reading to say, 'Did I mention that I asked Mrs E to air the beds in the spare rooms? You won't have to venture out again tonight.' Since this was not unexpected, having become customary on convivial occasions such as this, the other two simply nodded their thanks. The Teapot Man, taking advantage of the pause, added more coal to the grate.

After reading for a few more minutes, Mr Pixum spoke. 'Well, my friends, this is not good. The hand is unclear in many places but I think I have the gist of it.'

'Go on,' said the fox, 'I'm all ears.'

'You may not feel quite so enamoured of your find when you know what it is you have acquired,' said Mr Pixum, 'It amounts to a very singular tale.'

'Then please enlighten us,' said The Teapot Man, rubbing his hands together.

'Well,' began Mr Pixum, 'This Humphrey Stipkins was a bookkeeper, described here as a dry sort of fellow. He worked on the accounts of one Jagg van der Boom, whom it seems, was a notorious trafficker in women-slaves and opium, among other things. Stipkins was never happy to be in his employ but, as so often happens, the lure of regular payment, from however disreputable a source, was too strong for an impoverished man to resist. He convinced himself that the end justified the means. It appears that Van der Boom seldom visited Stipkins at his premises (the location of which, incidentally, he refrains from giving), sending his lieutenant, a queer character by the name of Nikodeemus Hackwell, to and fro with documents, payments and receipts. Inevitably, as time went by, Stipkins succumbed to temptation.'

'Surely such a clandestine livelihood would have no need of any visible transactions, for obvious reasons,' said The Teapot Man.

'The disreputable side of things went on behind a façade of respectability. Van der Boom owned several legitimate companies, including a shipping line, through which the illicit funds were filtered,' said Mr Pixum, 'and it was with these accounts that Stipkins became creative. He fiddled the daybooks and ledgers, all the while keeping a separate set of accounts for himself, in order to keep track of his embezzlements. This went very much in Stipkins' favour for several years. For this reason, he began to take the extra income (which, by the way, was considerable) for granted. Van der Boom's suspicions were aroused by an increasing number of shortfalls, which, presumably, were noticeable because Stipkins had become blasé and hadn't bothered to disguise them effectively. One day, Van der Boom and Hackwell called at his office unannounced. Needless to say, they soon had the truth of it from his own lips. They ransacked the premises and found the evidence in the duplicate ledgers. Retribution was swift—and horrible. In fact, it was horribly creative. Perhaps Van der Boom decided to mete out poetic justice by subjecting Stipkins to a creative punishment to match his creative bookkeeping?

'Stipkins was immediately imprisoned. Van der Boom owned a great many warehouses and other buildings with cellars and attics, any of which would serve the purpose of escape-proof cell. Stipkins had no idea where he was held. The first punishment was starvation. The second was to deprive the prisoner of drinking water until he was barely alive. It tells us something about the man's will to live that he survived to this point. Worse was to come. Instructed by Van der Boom, Hackwell came into the cell with two identical jugs of water. He told Stipkins one of them was poisoned and even a sip would mean agonising death, the other was pure spring water. He then proceeded to switch the jugs around, moving them quickly in an attempt to confuse Stipkins's eye. To make things more difficult, Hackwell turned his back on the prisoner and switched jugs—or not—making it impossible for Stipkins to be sure which jug was which. "Would you like a cool drink, Humphrey?" teased Hackwell as he took his leave, "Go ahead, choose your jug."

'Stipkins was half insane with thirst by this time, alternately gibbering and screaming.'

'I would smash a window with a chair and climb down the bed sheets,' interrupted Mr Fox.

'It says here, "He would have smashed a window with a chair and climbed down the bed sheets, had there been window or bed sheets in his prison. Alas, the window was bricked up and the only chair was riveted to the floor. He had but a straw mattress on which to repose, without linen of any kind." It goes on to say that, somehow, he managed to resist the water for two more days. During that time his *materiality* weakened further but his mind experienced peculiar moments of clarity. It says his body began to change around this time. In a mad vision, he saw things, things that would make sense eventually. In one of those moments of clarity, he saw the scene in which Hackwell teased him with the water, played out before his mind's eye in great detail. It was slowed down. He could study all of Hackwell's movements. He knew he was going to survive! Then Hackwell turned his back. He was no better off. He replayed the memory, taking it back a little farther. He saw himself screaming and tearing his greasy hair. He saw a hair fly from his mad fingers and stick to the rim of a jug. He heard Hackwell's voice telling him which of the jugs held pure water.'

'*Incroyable!*' exclaimed Mr Fox, 'He was saved by his delirium.'

'Not as you might have concluded,' Mr Pixum said, 'though he did indeed avoid the poison. The first thing he did after making his discovery, was to pour away the pure spring water. He let it trickle slowly through the floorboards. "It must be remembered," the narrator says, "that he was only a beginner at that time. The effort required to abstain from drinking the water was almost his undoing. He could feel the very timbers of his mind begin to crack. He held fast, even with his feeble, starved limbs shaking with frustration. When Nikodeemus arrived, he found a desiccated corpse. He saw the remaining jug and knew Stipkins had drunk from the poison. He laughed. He drank from the jug. Then Stipkins laughed. The last thing Nikodeemus Hackwell saw as he died a horrible death, was Stipkins's laughing face. Why did Hackwell drink from a jug he knew to contain mere springwater? To celebrate inflicting a cruel demise upon Stipkins? I believe he was mocking his victim in death." The tale begins to take a sinister turn beyond this point, I'm afraid.'

'I thought it had made that turn some time ago,' said Mr Fox, 'I'm not sure I have the heart to hear more of it tonight.'

'Come, Bertie, we can't leave it now,' said Mr Pixum, 'We may as well get it over with. Here, put aside your wine and take something stronger.'

Armed with large brandies, the trio braced themselves for the final chapter of Stipkins's tale. Mr Pixum turned over a page.

'Stipkins took the keys from Hackwell's corpse but before he let himself out of the room in which he'd been imprisoned, he swapped his clothes with those of Hackwell and dragged Hackwell's remains into a corner, where, should anyone take a casual glance, the candlelight would reach but poorly. Barely able to hold himself upright, he made his way down a flight of stairs by the light of the candle, hoping to leave whatever building he was in as quickly as possible. From below, he heard footsteps approaching. He snuffed the candle and shuffled into a pitch black room to hide, waiting inside until whoever it was passed by, then, by touch alone, descended the next flight of steps. At the bottom, although in total darkness, he sensed he was in a large room. All he could do was navigate around the walls, using his sense of touch to guide him, hoping to find a doorway.

'After groping his way along two sides of the room space, the plaster crumbling in his hands, his fingers found cloth. Thinking it was a curtain, he pulled it aside and found . . . buttons. A dark lantern was opened, revealing to Stipkins the figure of Jagg Van der Boom. Never on a human face had he beheld such a cruel smile. Paralysed with shock, Stipkins remained in place, his cheek pressed against the dank wall, one hand outstretched, his fingers grasping Van der Boom's waistcoat button. Without hesitating, Van der Boom coshed him to the ground.

'Stipkins awoke to a familiar sight: his prison room. You will remember it says he was only a beginner? Well, he had plenty of practice in the following weeks. Van der Boom continued to starve him. Hackwell's carelessness had cost him dearly. His new guard was Samuel Croom. Stipkins found this man to be a good deal sharper than his predecessor but if he kept quiet and did as he was told, Croom treated him fairly, at least for the time being.

'What do you think he was practising? Well, it seems this devious bookkeeper had discovered how to live without water. The writer says Stipkins doesn't mean he could actually remain alive without water at that point, that would come later. As the weeks passed, Stipkins and Croom struck up a companionable relationship. It grew out of boredom: Croom was almost as much a prisoner as was Stipkins. As Stipkins's new skill developed, so did he form a plan. He still had a large fortune hidden away; he would use it to make his escape. One night, speaking through the door, he said to Croom, "I have a proposition . . ."'

Mr Pixum could see that this narrative had taken his friends away from the cosy room and placed them into the dismal world of the prisoner. To cheer them up, he suggested a timely replenishment of brandy. Once this was achieved, he continued.

'The only drawback in Stipkins's plan was that it required time to put into effect. Croom was amenable to the scheme: after all, every man in *their* world had his price, and Stipkins was shrewd enough to name it precisely, not a penny more. One day, Croom came into the prison room, plainly agitated. Van der Boom had issued new instructions. His fury had abated not at all and he was determined to retrieve his missing fortune. Croom was to—I won't go into too much detail—torture Stipkins into revealing where he'd hidden the money. Van der Boom had commanded him to . . . hmm, this is distasteful, I warn you . . . fix a wooden clamp over Stipkins's head, with two glass vials, one each side, covering his ears. He was to remove certain . . . extremities from Stipkins's person and place them in equal amounts, along with some flesh-eating beetles of the species *Dermestes maculatus*, into the vials. Croom explained that Van der Boom's idea was that the prisoner would be forced to listen to the beetles as they ate his parts. The experience would persuade Stipkins to talk. Stipkins knew that once he gave Van der Boom the information, that would be the end of him.

'For distinctly different reasons, neither Croom nor Stipkins wanted this to transpire. They discussed the matter at length. Croom informed Van der Boom the torture was in progress. The upshot was that their only hope was to implement their plan a great deal more swiftly than was safe, but it was the only way. Should Van der Boom pay a surprise visit . . . But Croom couldn't simply help Stipkins escape: there were more men downstairs that he had no hope of circumventing, besides, he was a married man with a family. He couldn't live as a fugitive. In short, they carried out the plan with alacrity. After only a fortnight, Croom left the building carrying . . .' Mr Pixum leaned forward and tapped the box. '. . . this.'

'The craftsmanship is excellent considering the time and the materials,' said The Teapot Man.

'What do you mean?' asked Mr Fox, 'What was the plan?'

'I think we are talking about a very singular kind of desiccation?' The Teapot Man surmised.

'We are indeed,' said Mr Pixum. 'Stipkins consciously desiccated himself by stages. Croom, a genuine craftsman, carried out the binding and the carpentry.' He placed the book and the vial back into the box and closed the lid. 'I deliberately did not show you what I found in the back pages. Nor shall I.'

'*Par la théière bleue de Bacchus!*' Mr Fox's jaw sagged. 'You can't mean . .?'

Mr Pixum and The Teapot Man nodded.

So swiftly did Mr Fox move that it was over before either of his companions could so much as speak. He dragged the heavy box to the window, pulled up the sash and heaved the thing out into the night. He returned to his chair out of breath, snatched up his glass and drained it. 'Please forgive me,' he said, 'for bringing that thing into your house.'

The gas jets flickered in the breeze and a few snowflakes blew inside. Mr Pixum strode over to the window and closed it, then, opening a cupboard, he removed a handful of candles and proceeded to place them about the room, lighting them with a spill as he did so.

'Let us have a pipe and a think,' he said, 'But first I have something else to add to the story.' He settled himself into his armchair, pipe and tobacco ready on the side table.

'You must be wondering what the rest of the plan entailed. It was this: Croom was to take the box away. He would tell Van der Boom that he found the lock picked and Stipkins gone. The men downstairs would attest that Croom had left by himself. How Stipkins had escaped he would leave them to work out. It would probably remain a mystery. Shortly afterwards he would leave Van der Boom's employ, hopefully on good terms. After a few months had elapsed, Croom would reconstitute Stipkins and receive his share of the spoils, *QED*.'

'There was a flaw?' The Teapot Man smiled as he lit his pipe.

'Just how can a man desiccate himself and then be reconstituted? This is biologically impossible, obviously. I'll make a guess that Stipkins somehow, in the far reaches of his extremity, discovered something extra. Let's say he accidentally tapped into that something that is way beyond the reach of average minds—and utilised it. How would that work? I'm not sure. Maybe he translated the main part of himself into that realm that is beyond time and space, leaving only his mortal clay, his elemental remains, behind. Perhaps he left a door open between his essential self and his dust? We'll never know. If I were going to work on something similar, I wouldn't begin or end as Stipkins did. His method is brutal and inexact. It lacks elegance. Though given the circumstances and the fact that he used knowledge picked up on the fly, as it were, he did remarkably well, I have to say. We must also admire Croom's skills as a craftsman.

'Croom wrote the book, of course. He knew the whole story direct from Stipkins. And since Croom wrote it, he could only remain anonymous. Why he made a record of the deed, I don't know. Perhaps he hoped it might fall into the hands of someone capable of completing the operation. The flaw, as you so rightly observe, Teapot Man, was in the matter of reconstitution. Stipkins, presumably in haste, omitted to give any instructions to Croom. A very clever plan foiled by something so glaringly obvious! Or perhaps Stipkins *did* inform Croom and Croom wasn't listening or he forgot. Perhaps the method was so obvious to Stipkins, he presumed it would be obvious to Croom? Or more likely, he reneged on their deal; after all, he may have feared Stipkins revived would be spotted and captured, there would always be the risk that, tortured, he would reveal Croom's involvement. He would never know peace. He had Stipkins's money . . . '

'I wonder how Fadder Regoat came by the box?' asked Mr Fox.

'Perhaps you should wonder who Regoat really is,' murmured The Teapot Man.

'Oh no,' groaned the fox, 'The carving on the box. I thought it looked familiar. Neurological structures, ganglia.'

Mr Pixum lit a spill from the fire. 'Something is bothering me,' he said, puffing on his pipe. 'I believe we have some unfinished business. I shall not rest easy until . . . Well, I think you can guess? Time enough for a pipe first, though.'

Twenty minutes later, the Feathers of Fate, wrapped for the cold, arrived in the hall. Mr Pixum was about to open the front door when Mrs Enderby bustled out of the scullery.

'It's a strange thing, Mr P. Very strange. I can't see 'ow I could've gorn an' lorst it, y'see?' It was unlike Mrs Enderby to admit to such a failing.

'Lost what?' asked Mr Pixum.

'I was sweepin' snow an' puttin' salt on the front doorstep when I spied it. I thought "That's worth a pretty penny to anybody," so I fetched it in. It was lyin' in the snow, like somebody 'ad dropped it there. I saw young Mr Fox, beggin' yer pardon, sir, bring it in with 'im when 'e came. 'Ow it got outside I don't know.'

All three companions stared at her. 'Wot? *I* never took it out, I swear!'

'Calm yourself,' said The Teapot Man, 'We have no doubts about your probity, you can rest assured of that.'

'What did you do with it?' asked Mr Fox.

'I brushed the snow off it. It was 'eavy, like. It was damp so I put it on top o' the oven, which was still a bit warm from me bakin'. I thought it would be alright ter put it on somethin' warm, long as it was not 'ot. Ter dry it out, like? Did I do right, Mr P?'

'You certainly did!' replied Mr Pixum, 'Then what happened?'

'Nothin' 'appened, sir. I came back from tidyin' up the scullery and saw it was gawn! Nothin' there but a funny bottle—and this!' She held out a brass button. Mavis Enderby was on the verge of tears. 'I was jest comin' up ter tell yer, when yer come down.'

'Thank you, Mrs E, you're a marvel!'

'I am?'

Mr Pixum and his friends marched to the door and found it unbolted.

Snow had almost covered Mrs Enderby's work; the steps would require another good sweeping in the morning. There was not too much recent snow, however, to obliterate the prints of bare feet leaving the house.

Mr Fox pushed by the other two and peered down the street, his eyes following the indentations in the virgin quilt as they receded along the pavement into the cold and dark distance.

Behind the open door, Mrs Enderby wailed.

'Owww! Somebody's taken my bestest coat from the peg!'

Mr Fox said, 'Now *there's* a coat that means something to someone.'

The Crispness of a Camel

How Mr Pixum, The Teapot Man and Mr Fox, together with Mavis Enderby (Mr P's housekeeper and cook), and sundry other guests, may have spent a particular Yuletide at Mr Pixum's great house, Westrum Powers, in the East of England; and how an unexpected (though distinguished) guest coped with what befell.

> Unique crystalline symmetry makes
> Multitudes of moonlit dancing flakes,
> Floating down about Westrum's gables,
> Observatory, barn, smithy and stables.
> Without 'twas Winter's eve so serene;
> Within 'twas a flickering, dream-lit scene.

A certain Teapot Man rails against his fate (to no avail).

[Bertie, I take exception to this last line. TPM.]

[Be a sport! It's a mere jape. B. Fox.]

> Bells on his teapot,
> Clad all in motley,
> So mad he could hop;
> He piped up hotly,
> 'I look like a Fool!'
> (Persuaded was he
> To dress thus for Yule:
> A Fool he must be!)

[I see you've puffed up yourself well enough. 'Slobbery of tongue,' I would have said. TPM.]

> E'er the same, year upon year, his charm
> Glinting with rascally fire in his gaze,
> Though he meant the coy maidens no harm,
> Conjured their wits and set them amazed,
> Mr Fox, so silvery of tongue,
> Had captured their hearts one by one.

With garlands of green
Ivy and holly
The hall had ne'er been
Bedecked quite so jolly.
Beside the hearth's blaze
With wine and a pipe
The Master sat mazed
And grinned at a gype.*

*An amusing
thought.

The cauldron steamed as Mrs E stirred
Milk of Paradise and honey-dew—
The kitchen, replete with basted bird,
Goodly roast beef and venison stew,
Boasted aromas delightfully appetising.
Cook's face reddened: the heat was rising!

*The pace
quickens; metre
and rhyme fly
out of the
window.*

Rat-tat! The door boomed throughout the hall!
'Up ter me elbows! On sitch a night!'
Mrs E worried and waddled and all
And drew back the bolt. 'Oh wot a sight!'
Informing the Master of this guest,
She asked what she should do for the best.
Mrs E asked Mr P,

*Balthasar, last of
the three Magi,
pays a visit to
Westrum.*

'Are you at 'ome to a Horiental guest
Wearin' wrappin's and wrappin's
And *wrappin's* of clawth?'

'Make him at home, as at home he can be!
Tell him my hat I do doff fig'ratively!'

Three Wise Men rode into the West,
Their mystery to find,
For they had taken a solemn oath:
'Find something good or dine.'

Going separate ways, off they tramelled,
Along bustling routes and roads less-camelled.
With merely a star (but no maps to guess from)
They could not have known:
All paths lead to Westrum.

Thus Balthasar embarked on an heroic tour
For he was third of the "We Three Kings".
The other two wizards were Caspar and Melchior;
They were three and wise and knew things.

When they set out "From Orient Are"
By astronomy and logic were they ruled,
They intended to follow Procyon, their guiding star:
Pixum's crystal sphere (a mere notion) had them
fooled.

The Master of Westrum Powers is unrepentant.

'An alchemist's trick; a chemical toy,
It floats on high—to steer here by,
Set in Procyon's quadrant by chance;
Should its light bring anyone joy
So what if it led "We Three Kings" a dance?'

Hitching his camel to Mr P's "star,"
The Magus has wander'd and wander'd
And *wander'd* the waste
For an aeon all told—he wasn't in haste—
And arrived, (immortal?), at Pixum's portal.

Mr Pixum thinks aloud - and instructs his housekeeper regarding the new arrival.

'Not another fool upon a dromedary!
Oh not another. The third of the three.
How did he organise his ridiculous itinerary?
Oh, put the humps in the stable
And the food in the larder,
The gifts upon the table.
And settle the un-wise one
'Pon his un-magic rug,
Serve him roast parsnips
And wine from a jug!'

<table>
<tr><td>Mr Pixum, Master
of Westrum
Powers, offers
words of
encouragement.</td><td>'Ho! Minstrels! Ho! Jongleurs!
Put some hum in the fiddles
And some row in the drums!
Make merry forthwith
Lest I griddle thy thumbs!'</td></tr>
</table>

<table>
<tr><td>Glazed meats
glister on the
sideboard along
with steaming
roast parsnips and
sweetmeats
aplenty!
Candied angelica,
jellicoe cherries,
custard and
gingerbread men.
Cornucopius
amounts of
everything:
meddlars,
tangerines, quinces,
pippins, walnuts,
filberts, chestnuts,
truckles of cheese,
pomegranates,
cinnamon, cloves,
loaves, mulled
wine, mead, rum
and brandy.</td><td>Teapot Man, Jester, Burlesquer and Fool,
Calimps and calooms up and down the great room,
Froddling the guests with bells and with brooms,
(Oh, ticklish toucan!)
Juggling crystalline ginger and barleysugar twists,
And balancing pomegranates on the backs of his
wrists.
With ribald asides he gives pick-a-back rides,
Tells lies, old riddles, tales of curved ghosts
And slips into pockets: chestnuts, roast.

A boar's head, glistening, is piped to the table,
The sideboards listing 'neath entremets and courses,
English roast beef, pepper and horse-radish sauces,
Venison haunch, rabbit pie,
Mincemeat served with ergot of rye,
Plum pudding by blue flames fondl'd.

Balthasar feasted upon pheasant and stuffing,
On nutmeg, candlewax, fieldmice and puffin
And lastly, roast camel.</td></tr>
</table>

<table>
<tr><td>He mourns his
fabled camel.</td><td>'Aesop the camel! My boyhood friend—
Such faith to stay beneath me unto the end.
Forsooth, in life, he rarely smelled great,
And of camels he was ne'er the best looking.
Now a gourmet's delight served 'pon a plate:
An aroma to die for, now he's been cooking!
Transformed into meat he's a sizzling beast,
His crackling's the apex of my humptyback feast!'</td></tr>
</table>

Mr P comments:
To each his own.

'Oh! *Merry* crispness!' thought he.
A stirring of conscience beset Mrs E.
In her cook's nips muddle:
'Put the food in the stable
And the gifts in the larder,
The 'umps on the spit.

In the hall,
firelight flutters,
candlelight shivers
on the table and
sconces, casting
leery shadows,
bringing ancestral
portraits to life
and busts to
mutter.

Oh, that was it!
Oh, what a fuddle!
Should've think'd 'arder . . .
(But my gravy was a *glory*!)' thought she.

At one end of the hall stood a bedizened fir
Festooned with candles, sweetmeats and myrrh.
On the tip, the top, the very treetop,
Perched the familiar, peculiar and mystical Teapot.

In the mouldings
on the ceiling,
spiders dance in
formation and
tiny demons
bimber and squeak.
Minstrels sweat
out merriment,
utilising wind,
string, brass and
skin.
Salamanders dart
in and out of the
fireplace.

To The Teapot Man, the Jester, the Persifleur,
Pixum suggested that, just for a dare,
'Scale the fir, my friend, scale the tree,
Retrieve your Crown and you'll
Once more be free—and furthermore—
With Crown of pot, like as not,
You're no more Fool but King of Yule!'

In gratitude, The
Teapot Man
pours a glass of
wine, hands it to
Mr Fox, then
savours his very
special tea and
proposes a toast.
He then removes
his motley crown
and replaces it
with his
accustomed
teapot. Mr Fox
pitches the
"Motleypot" at the
tip of the fir,
where it perches
perfectly.

The fox, pleased with his evening of repartee,
And fresh from a jug of punch—or three
And full of cheer, unfecularity and glee,
Insisted with zest he'd relieve the Jester
As he was the bester to scale the tree!

Up like a chimp or mischievous imp,
He plucked up the pot—'Bugger! It's hot!'
And, with reynardly grace, he slid down to earth,
Scattering candles, candies, frankincense and mirth.
'I thank thee friend and fellow seeker;
Without thee, life would be obliquer:
Take this I offer; we'll clink vessels in toast—
"To camels all: one hump or two; quick or roast!"'

Appreciating this sentiment, Balthasar the Mage
Rose to his feet, took centre stage
'A brief recital, learned on my travels
I would offer to this happy throng.'

Mr Pixum gives
his permission.

'Hold forth in welcome! Hold forth as guest!
Pile revel 'pon revels ere the wassail unravels!
In my breast, in my cups, I'm desirous of drama.
I believe I speak for the rest!'

Balthasar asks
for silence
before he speaks.

'As honoured guest I make a request:
I won't speak in this din! Pray be calmer!
Ah, I'm obliged, fellows all—I begin.

† *'Our plummeting*
flagellant dons a
tetrahedral helmet,
slips a slightly
scratched carving of
a frog into his pocket,
gathers his wits and
gives chase.'

'Upser rip toon foursquare,†
Rabnactery,‡ stillbeeth and clement,
It slunk through the snicket
Furtively mallorsk, where
Into a fogue impediment⁕
Footling Peterkin pick it;
Hermiment, mauders and stegging . . .'

‡ *Abstruse*
reference to
breathing through
the ears.

⁕*It hides in a*
cellar.

Scores more of (it seemed, similar) verses,
Droned on 'mid suffering and curses,
And finally came to an end.
It was clear by the tear
In Balthasar's eye
That in his recital the depths of his soul
Had been bared.
Equally clear from the lack of applause:
Not one of his audients cared.

Here Mr Fox
presents himself
somewhat out of
character -
(continued opposite.)

'Dash my wig!' the fox declared,
'Thou hast killed these revels dead!
Should the Green Knight appear tonight,
Forsooth, he shall have your head!'

As head of the house Mr Pixum bestirred,
Was about to give voice to restraint
When, as if summoned,
 a knock on the door was heard!
There stood the Green Knight—
That *very* Green Knight—
He stood very green in the night.
And how very *green* was his paint!

The fox quoth in rage, 'This mountebank Mage
Shall forfeit his head to your sword!'
Sir Bertilak de Hautdesert*
Felt it incumbent on him to assert
That the magus should have the first hack.
'Fie!' the fox cried, 'The rules don't apply
To any Mage whose prominent quality is *lack*!'

'As a guest of my house I cannot allow
A hair of his head to be harmed.
On another occasion, instead of abrasion
This very same crowd would be charmed.'

The Knight relaxed, the fox stood down,
The Knight delivered his gift.
'These hogsheads of ale that rest in my dray
Will give flagging spirits a lift
And cider in flagons that stand in my wagon
Will blow the cold Winter away!'

Hands were shaken, drink was taken;
Goodwill was more than restored.
The company, with minstrelsy,
 Danced and sang and roared.
'A toast!' cried the King of Yule,
"May harmony and merriment hold sway
To banish all drear for the rest of the year
And blow the cold Winter away!"'

Notes on *The Crispness of a Camel*

Mr Pixum declared he would like to see this tale in verse. Furthermore, he said it would be written by all three Feathers of Fate: himself of course, The Teapot Man and Mr Bertie Fox, each contributing several verses as their fancy took them.

My role has been simply to edit the sheaf of crumpled and blotted papers I received.

Where instances of obscurity reign supreme, I have attempted to render the spelling and language into standard English although in several instances no equivalent words exist. On these occasions, to avoid cumbersome translation, I have decided to preserve the rhyming, such as it is, at the expense of clarity.

Mr Pixum has kindly provided the marginalia. For epistolary purposes, some printable comments of a personal nature are included by all three, [shown thus].

Mr Pixum assures me I have assembled the verses in the correct sequence.

Any doubts I may harbour as to the veracity of this assurance do not necessarily arise from the confusion in his expression and the vague half-smile he gave when I asked. Nor does any doubt I may have that he gave my proof more than a cursory glance stem from the fact that Mr Pixum failed to strike out this sentence.

WJB

Acknowledgements

Huge thanks to: Harvey and Francine Moulden for over-seeing Mr Fox's French dialogue; Sarah Cherry for her constructive comments on the whole work-in-progress and for her diligent (and amazingly patient) proof-reading; Phil Rickman for his encouragement; Mr Pixum for clarifying at least a few of my queries. All errors are mine. WJB

Trippers

On the road in England 1971... A very English Kerouac set to a 'Withnail & I' scale, this book is based upon the author's personal experiences in the summer of 1971. Bill Booker wakes up to the fact that he's a lonely stranger amongst his so-called friends and, spurred on by the need to sort his head out, he sets off on a journey accompanied by some new friends, roving from place to place, wandering through his memories, dreams and reflections, cadging cigarettes from strangers, soaring upon hallucinogenic wings, devouring egg and chips in back street cafés, haunted by a pair of apparitions, his insecurity and his friend's abominable feet... This is Bill's quest to find his personal Grail... Bill Booker's unique outlook, thought-provoking comments and observations on life will appeal to anyone who enjoys reading about personal discovery, personal relationships and to every new generation that wants to know what hippies/freaks/acidheads really got up to in the early 1970s and anyone who lived through that time who's ready for a nostalgia fix.
ISBN: ISBN-10: 1908248963
ISBN-13: 978-1908248961

Trippers Amazon review excerpts:

"Thoroughly recommend this to anyone who wants to settle down and think about things. Society, politics, the meaning of life, love, and religion, you name it, this book will take you through it. Beautiful."
★★★★★ (Chanatkins)

The Yellow Booke Volume III

M. Grant Kellermeyer
(Collection featuring my tale '*Mrs Ellsworth's Cakes*')
ISBN-10: 1532842775
ISBN-13: 978-1532842771

"An excellent volume of strange and darksome stories."
★★★★ (Michael Adams)

"Bill's quest and understanding about light, love, and oneness, is like reading one of those books about Buddhist experiences and the connectedness of all existence, leaving one with a sense of awe and positivity."
★★★★★ (The Bub)